# The Story of Viga-Glum

Translated from the Icelandic by

## Sir Edmund Head

*First published in 1866*

Published by Left of Brain Books

ISBN 978-1-397-66978-0

*First Edition*

# PUBLISHER'S PREFACE

**About the Book**

"Viga-Glums saga is one of the Icelanders' sagas. It tells of a chieftain who kills several people and tries to cover his guilt. It is believed to have been written in the 13th century."

*(Quote from wikipedia.org)*

# CONTENTS

1

# DEDICATION

### To Iceland

Hail, Isle! with mist and snowstorms girt around,
Where fire and earthquake rend the shatter'd ground--
Here once o'er furthest ocean's icy path
The Northmen fled a tyrant monarch's wrath:
Here, cheer'd by song and story, dwelt they free,
And held unscath'd their laws and liberty.

# PREFACE

I HAVE heard the question asked, "What interest can attach to the language and literature of a small and remote island, the inhabitants of which never exceeded 60,000 in number?" The population of Iceland has always been insignificant, and its territory barren, but we must recollect what the race was, which this population represented, and whose language it is that has come down to us as a living tongue, on this half desert spot in in the Northern Ocean. The Sagas, of which this tale is one, were composed for the men who have left their mark in every corner of Europe, and whose language and laws are at this moment important elements in the speech and institutions of England, America, and Australia. There is no page of modern history in which the influence of the Northmen and their conquest must not be taken into account--Russia, Constantinople, Greece, Palestine, Sicily, the coasts of Africa, Southern Italy, France, the Spanish Peninsula, England, Scotland, Ireland, and every rock and island round them, have been visited, and most of them at one time or another, ruled by the men of Scandinavia. The motto on the sword of Roger Guiscard was a proud one--

Appulus et Calaber Siculus mihi servit, et Afer."
(Raumer, Hohenstaufen, b. i. circa 473).

The remoteness or insignificance of Iceland, therefore, affords no adequate measure of the interest which belongs to its language, its literature, and its history. All this has been fully discussed by Mr. Laing in his prefaces to the Heimskringla, and by Mr. Dasent in the essay prefixed to his excellent translation of the Nial's Saga. But there is another point of view in which these Icelandic stories possess a great and peculiar interest in relation to their history of literature. Taken altogether, they are the first prose literature which exists in any modern language spoken by the people.

Notwithstanding the fact that Monsieur Jourdain had talked prose for forty years without knowing it, good composition in prose is a product of the human intellect of far slower growth than good poetry. Imagination and metre have always been in advances of plain facts and prose.

We admit that Greek prose writers existed in the sixth century before Christ, but that was long after the birth of Greek poetry; and prose writing ripened only in the time of Herodotus, when very little more was known about the author of the Homeric songs than we moderns know at this day.

In what country except Scandinavia, or in what other modern living language of Europe did there exist, in the elevenths century, a literature embracing history and prose-fiction?

No doubt there were translations into Anglo-Saxon from the Latin, by Alfred, of an earlier date, but there was in truth no vernacular literature. I cannot name any work in High or Low German prose which can be carried back to this period. In French prose-writing cannot be said to have begun before the time of Villehardouin (1204), and Joinville (1202). Castilian prose certainly did not commence before the time of Alfonso X. (1252). Don Juan Manuel, the author of the "Conde Lucanor," was not born till 1282. The Cronica General de Espana was not composed till at least the middle of the thirteenth century. About the same time the language of Italy was acquiring that strength and softness which were destined to appear so conspicuously in the prose of Boccaccio, and the writers of the next century.

Burt "Are hinn frodi," who is said by Snorri to have first committed these Sagas to writing, was born in 1067, and it must be supposed on reasonable grounds that the earlier ones had assumed their present form before the end of the twelfth century. It should be remembered, too, that the number of these compositions is very large, and that they contain both history and fiction. The reader will find a list of Icelandic works in Mr. Laing's book, already referred to. Our existing MSS of them cannot be assigned to a date earlier than the fourteenth century.

Of these sagas that of Viga-Glum, now translated, is probably one of the earliest. Bishop Müller says of it, in his "Saga Bibliothek" (Copenhagen, 1817, b. i. 78): "This Saga conains important contributions ito the history of manners, legislation, and religious ideas. It is composed in the pure old language, and is without doubt one of the earliest written narratives. The events are true. The most important persons and acts are spoken of in the Landnama. Glum himself is named in the Valnaliot's Saga, in the Kristni Saga, and in the Landnama. His quarrels with Viga Skuta are told with more detail in the Sagas of the latter. Glum's son, Vigfuss, is mentioned in many Sagas, and in the Heimskringla, in Olaf Tryggvesen's history, chapter 45 (Laing's Transl. vol. i. p. 410). His nephew, Thorvald Tafalld, who supported him in his fights, has also been made the subject of a special little narrative, which is to be found in Olaf Tryggvesen's Saga. The annals mention one of Glum's exploits under the year 942 or 944. Asgrim, the son of Ellidagrim, who is named in this Saga, is known to us also in the Nial's Saga, Floamanna Saga, and Kristni Saga. Einar, Gudmund's brother, is often mentioned, especially in the Liosvetninga Saga."

Einar, here referred to by Bishop Müller, was a remarkable person in Icelandic history. He was the brother of Gudmund the Powerful, and the direct descendant of Helga, the sister of Ingald, Glum's grandfather. When Olaf, King of Norway, wanted to obtain the island of Grimsö with a view to encroaching the independence of Iceland, Einar addressed to his countrymen one of the simplest and most striking speeches ever made on behalf of freedom. He counselled them to have nothing to do with the king, except in the way of gifts or voluntary presents which could not be mistaken for tribute. This speech will be found in Mr. Laing's Heimskringla, vol. ii. p. 188.

With regard to the intrinsic merits of the narrative, the reader must judge for himself. The picture of society which it presents to us is not one of pastoral simplicity and repose, but the actors in it are real men and women, not merely lay figures, and the events are for the most part those of every-day life. Bloodshed and violence are common, and a man's consideration in the community depends mainly on his won courage and on his wealth yet the condition of things contrast favourably with that prevailing in most countries at a far later date under the fuedal system. The bulk of the population were free; they made their own laws, and executed them themselves, and we see among them the working of those principles of constitutional freedom which in most countries of Europe have long since perished. One peculiarity too they have which is especially interesting to us. They exhibit in a most remarkable degree that idolatry for forms of law, which sometimes causes the substance of justice to be disregarded as secondary to the form, but which, on the other hand, in our own country, has perhaps more than once saved the kernel by preserving the husk, when both would otherwise have perished. I believe it is a curious fact that the Normans retain to the present day a reputation for litigiousness as compared with other French provinces.

Viga-Glum, or "Murdering Glum," the hero of this story, is not by any means a perfect character, even when measured by the standards of the time in which he lived; but the author tells us that for twenty years he was the first man in Eyjafirth, and for twenty years more there was no better man there. He is described as one who was naturally indolent, shy, and moody; but when once he could be brought to act, his courage and determination were indomitable. he was thoroughly unscrupulous; neither blood nor false oaths stood in his way when he had to achieve a purpose. It might be said of him, as of Autolycus, the grandfather of Ulysses (Od. xix. 395). His humour is sometimes childish, as is the story of Kálf; and sometimes savage, as when he asks the wife to put a stitch into his cloak just before he turns round and kills her husband, apparently for no object but to show his thorough coolness and indifference. The finishing touch to this part of his character is added by the peculiarity, that whenever he was intent on slaying a man, he was apt to be seized with a fit of uncontrollable laughter which ended in tears.

There is something very striking too in the description of the old heathen, stone-blind, who hopes before he dies, yet to slay by treachery one at least of his enemies, and rides out to meet them with a drawn sword under his cloak.

Among the incidents of the story, that of Eyiolf killing the Berserker is to me particularly interesting. It is one of many such in the Sagas, as for instance in the Egil's Saga and the Grettir's Saga. Here we find the type of the old common-stock stories of romance about distressed damsels rescued by knights from giants' but we see this type exemplified in everyday life, as if it were something that might happen to any man the next morning; and as we are told in the Grettir's Saga it did happen very often in Norway when those pests of the society of that day, the Berserkers, were allowed to make their way in the world, and advance their fortunes as professional bullies. [1]

The story is not always intelligible unless the reader keeps in mind the personal relations of the actors, and I have therefore appended to the translation two or three pedigrees of the families to which they belonged. With regard to the Icelandic text it should be observed that there is but one manuscript of any value, the others being mere transcripts. The obscurities arising from this fact are especially felt in the scraps of poetry, which are often very difficult to make out. They have very little merit and I have done no more than paraphrase their general meaning; but they could not be omitted altogether, as in one or two cases the story turns upon their contents. In the prose narrative I have adhered to the original as closely as was consistent with my desire of presenting to the English reader a translation that could be read without being very stiff and tiresome, but I am by no means sure that I have attained this object.

I ought not to close this Preface without acknowledging the assistance which I have received from Mr. Dasent and especially from Mr. Vigfusson, the Editor of the "Eyrbyggia Saga," printed at Leipzig in 1864. Another friend, the Right Honourable Robert Lowe, has permitted me to prefix to this book a Greek Epigram of his addressed to Iceland, which is worthy of his reputation as a classical scholar. I only wish that his public occupations would allow us to profit by his acquirements in the language and literature of the North.

EDMUND HEAD

---

[1] See Grettir's Saga, chap. xix. 40.

London, December, 1865.

# CHAPTER I.

THERE was a man called Ingiald, who lived at Thverá, on the Eyjafirth; he was one of the original priests and a great chief, and he was already in years when this story begins. [1] Ingiald was married, and had two sons, Steinolf and Eyiolf, both right good men and fair to see. Ingiald himself was self-willed, reserved, hard to deal with, and obstinate. He cared little for merchants, and did not choose to submit to their arrogance. If he wanted anything from them, he preferred sending other people for it to going himself.

One summer a ship came into Eyjafirth, the master of which was named Hreidar: he was a man of great family, who had his home at Vorz in Norway, and was very courageous and very popular. Ingiald's son, Eyiolf, was often about the ship in the course of the summer, and he and Hreidar became great friends. Hreidar told him he should like to pass the winter here in some house, and from the report he had heard he should prefer that of Ingiald. Eyiolf said that such was not his father's wont, but still that he would see about it. When he came home, he spoke to his father and asked him to take the master of the

---

[1] It might have been better to keep the Icelandic term "Godi" in the text; for the civil duties of this functionary were more important than his priestly office. "One of the original priests" means one of the holders of a "Godord," or "Mannaforrad," from the time of the settlement of the island at the close of the ninths centry. On the nature of the Godi's office, see Mr. Dasent's Preface to the Nial's Saga, p. xlvi., and Maurer's "Enstehung des Isländischen Staats und seiner Verfassung" (München, 1852), ss. 82, 83, 89, etc. Compare also the subsequent note on the judicial proceedings.

ship into his house--that he was a good, worthy fellow--and pleaded strongly in his behalf. Ingiald replied, "If you have invited him already, what is the use of talking about it? I must bear my part in meeting the expense, and you must bear yours in taking all the trouble;" but he added that he had never had a foreigner staying with him before and that he was still not desirous of doing so. Then Eyiolf answered, "It has not yet been settled without your consent; but I have not had much share in the management of the house as yet, and it seems your will that I should not have much, if a guest is not to be received whom I have invited hither." "Well," said Ingiald, "you shall have your own way in this matter, and the master and one other man may come here. I shall make no charge, for your sake; but you must take all the trouble for them, and I will defray the cost." "I am well pleased," replied Eyiolf, "that so it should be."

Eyiolf went the next day, found Hreidar, and told him how matters stood, whereupon Hreidar expressed his satisfaction and betook himself, with his cargo, to Ingiald's house. A short time afterwards he learned that there was to be a great gathering there at Christmas. In the meantime Ingiald, though reserved, was on good terms with him.

One day Hreidar asked Ingiald to go into the outhouse where his cargo was; and when he went he invited him to choose whatever he liked out of his goods. Ingiald said that he did not wish to take any of his property, but acknowledged his liberality. Hreidar replied, "I have, however, thought of something that you may want from us. I have been in several of the best dwellings here in Eyjafirth, and I have seen none so good as this; but the hangings for your hall are not such as to surpass those of other people." So saying, he took from his chests a set of hangings of such quality that no better had ever come to Iceland, and gave them to Ingiald, who thanked him; and a friendly feeling was now established between them. In the course of the winter Eyiolf said that he should like to sail with Hreidar on his outward voyage, but Hreidar did not answer him very readily. "Why," says Eyiolf, "will you not take me with you? Do you not like me?" "I like you right well, but your father will not approve of such a return for his hospitality, and I should not like to repay his kindness by taking away a son who is such a credit to him. If he approves, I shall willingly take you with me, and be truly thankful for your going."

Now the traders prepared for their voyage, and when they were ready, Eyiolf again asked Hreidar about taking him out: he told him what he wanted, and how he did not mean to act in this matter against his father's wishes. Afterwards, he told his father how anxious he was to go, and what had passed between himself and Hreidar. Ingiald said there were few such mean as Hreidar to be found, "and what with your own conduct and his tried worth, I shall allow you to go, for I am sure you had better make the voyage with him than with any one else."

# CHAPTER II.

THEN they sailed and arrived in Norway; and Heidar laid before Eyiolf many schemes for disposing of himself, but he would not agree to anything which was proposed. "Well," said Hreidar, "what are your plans, then?" "I really do not know." "Will you not visit the king, or some of the other great men? You would, as a matter of course, be entitled to every assistance from us. (At this time Hacon, the ward of Athelstan, ruled in Norway.) [1] Such chiefs are the persons whom you ought to serve." Eyiolf answered, "I am not well fitted for a king's service; and though things might turn out as I should desire, yet I decline the proposal." Hreidar said, "What will you do, then?" "Why," replied Eyiolf, " do you shirk asking me to your own house? for that is what I want." "I do not like to offer you that which it is not good you should accept, and good alone ought you to have at my hands." "I am curious," said Eyiolf, "to know how this matter stands." "You shall know all about it," answered Hreidar, "although it befits me ill to speak of it. I have a brother named Ivar; we live together, and hold our property jointly, and are very fond of one another; but we are not of the same mind in one thing, for he cannot bear any Icelander; so that they are not safe where he is. He is out sea-roving all the summer; but when he comes home, he takes up his quarters in my house, with ten or twelve men, and every-

---

[1] The date asigned for this voyage of Eyiolf is 918, at which time Hacon, the ward of Athelstan, had not succeeded to the throne, but Harold Hárfagr was still king. See Laing's "Heimskringla," vol. i. p. 314. It is very possible that these words may have been inserted by some transcriber.

body there has to look to their wishes. All these fellows will be so ill-disposed towards you, that you would not in any way be comfortable there."

"I am very curious, said Eyiolf, "to learn what these men are like, and whatever happens, it will be no fault of yours, if you let the visit take place." Hreidar replied, "I owe this to my brother, seeing that he brings me home the excellent gifts which he does--not to let a difference arise between us on your account-- and I shall be very much vexed if they mock and insult you." "Ah! you want terribly to get out of having me at your house," remarked Eyiolf; "but how will he bear himself towards me--will he beat me?" "It will be something worse than beating; he has many ill-conditioned men with him, and they will put the worst construction on all you do or say." Eyiolf said, "That's no great trial. If a man knows it before, it is folly not to bear that sort of thing: that shall be no hindrance." Hreidar replied, "There is a difficulty both ways--you are my friend, and he is my brother, whom I love much."

The end of it was that Eyiolf went to stay at Hreidar's, on the promontory; and when Ivar was expected home, he put on a great fur cloak, which he wore every day; he was a tall man, and sat always at Hreidar's side.

# CHAPTER III.

NOW, when Ivar arrived, they went out to meet him as a mark of honour, and received him joyfully. Either brother then aksed the other for tidings and Ivar inquired of Hreidar where he had been through the winter. Hreidar told him he had been in Iceland, and then Ivar asked no more about the matter; "but tell me," said he, "is that great rough lump I see there a man, or is it some animal?" Eyiolf answered, "I am a man of Iceland, my name is Eyiolf, and I intend to be here all the winter." "I guess one thing," said Ivar; "we shall not be without mischief of some kind, if an Icelander is here." Hreidar replied, "If you deal badly with him, so that he cannot stay here, the affection between us, as near kinsmen, will suffer." "It was a bad voyage of yours to Iceland," said Ivar, "if we on that account are to be dependent on Icelanders, or cast off our own friends and kindred: nor do I know why you chose to visit that most hateful people; and then too you have escaped telling me what has happened to you." [1] "It is very different from what you suppose," said Hreidar; "there are many good fellows there." "Well," replied Ivar, "at any rate that rough and shaggy beast does not look particularly well on the high seat." But when he saw that his brother set great store by Eyiolf he did not speak so strongly as before against Icelanders. "What can I call him," said he, "except "Lump?'" and Eyiolf did

---

[1] Ivar considers it an aggravation of the annoyance caused by Eyiolf that his brother had visited a place which he hated and which he had no wish to hear anything about, and so they had not the pleasure of telling one another how they had fared during their absence.

not seem to object to the name; but they made the worst of everything that he did.

There was a man named Vigfuss, lord of the district of Vorz, the son of Sigurd, who was the son of Kari-Viking; and Vigfuss had a daughter, called Astrida. Hreidar and Ivar were great friends of Vigfuss, and they used to entertain one another alternate winters, at Christmas. At this time it was the turn of the brothers to prepare for the feast. In fact Hreidar had got everything ready, and had then to invite his guest. He asked Eyiolf to go with him, "for," said he, "I have no curiosity to try how they will behave towards you here." "I am not well," replied Eyiolf, "and I cannot go." That evening, when Hreidar was gone and they took their places, Ivar's companions exclaimed, "Now we shall amuse ourselves as we please, for old 'Lump' is left at home." "Nay," said Ivar, "we must think of something which befits us. Here we are, two brothers, holding our property jointly, and he has all the trouble of it, whilst I have none. This is a man to whom he wishes to be kind, and we act in such a way that he can scarcely stay here, but at the same time we have no fault to find with him. No man shall say anything injurious to him whilst Hreidar is absent." They replied it was just the time to have some sport. "No," said Ivar, "there is little true manhood in what you say. Every one waits on us here, and we have all the sport we choose, but others have the labour and care. If that man had killed my brother, I would not, for Hreidar's sake, do him any harm, and no one shall dare to make sport of him." He shall not be called 'Lump' any longer." In the morning Ivar spoke with Eyiolf: "Will you go into the wood with us and amuse yourself" He assented to this and went with them: they took to cutting down trees and carrying them home. Eyiolf had with him his sword and a hatchet. "I advise you, Icelander," said Ivar, "if our men go each his on way, that you get home before dark." So each man went his own way, and

Eyiolf went off by himself, and taking off his rough cloak, laid upon it the sword which he hand in his hand. Then he turned into the wood to amuse himself with his hatchet, and cut down the trees which he fancied. As the day advanced it came on to snow, and he thought of going home; but when he came to the spot where he had left his cloak it was gone, and the sword remained behind. He saw a track in the snow as if the cloak had been dragged along. A bear had come and carried off the cloak, but had hardly had strength to hold it off the ground, for it was a young bear, just come out of its lair, that had never killed a man. They Eyiolf went and saw the bear sitting before him, so he drew his sword and cut off its snout close to the eyes and took it home with him in his hand. Ivar came home first, missed Eyiolf, and exclaimed, "We have made a bad expedition of it, and we have done wrong in parting from our comrade in the wood, for he does not know his way in it. It is likely that there are wild beasts there, and considering the footing on which we have been with him, it would be much talked about, if he did not get safe back. I advise that we should go and look for him till we find him." When they got out before the door, there was Eyiolf coming to meet them, and Ivar greeted him well, and asked how he came to be covered with blood. Eyiolf showed them what he held in his hand, and Ivar said, "I fear you are wounded?" but he answered, "Don't trouble yourself about me; I have no hurt." Ivar exclaimed, "What folly it is to mock men whom we do not know! He has shown in this matter a courage which I doubt if any of us would come up to."

The following evening Hreidar came home, and Ivar asked him, "Why are you so moody, brother? Are you anxious about 'Lump?' How do you think I am likely to have dealt with him?" "No doubt," said Hreidar, "it is of some consequence how you have acted in this matter." "What will you give me, if I should be on the same terms with him as you are yourself?" "I will give you," answered Hreidar, "that gold ring which belongs to both of us and which you have long liked." Ivar replied, "I don't covet your property, but I shall for the future stand to him in the same relation as to yourself, and henceforth he shall sit by my side, and not by yours." Then both of them held Eyiolf in high honour, and felt that the place he sat in was worthily filled; and so it went on.

# CHAPTER IV.

NOW people came to the Christmas feast, and those who were to sit together were told off in messes of twelve. Lots were cast to see who should sit next to Astrida, the daughter of the chief Vigfuss, and Eyiolf always drew the lot for sitting by her side. No one observed that they talked together more than other persons did, but still men said that it was fated to come about in that way that he should marry her. The feast came to an end, after being celebrated with great splendour, and the guest were dismissed with presents. Eyiolf went sea-roving for four summers, and was held to be a very valiant man. He gained great reputation and much booty. It happened one winter that a certain Thorstein came to Vorz, who was a great friend of the brothers, and lived in the upland country. He told them of the strait he was in; how the Berserker, [1] who was called Asgaut, had challenged him to the "holmgang," because he had refused to give him his sister, and he asked them to

---

[1] It is hardly necessary to explain that the Berserkers were men who were ready to fight anybody, and who worked themselves into a frenzy by drugs or other means, as a North American savage does by his war-dance. They appear in some cases to have made a profession of challenging every one, to whose land, or wife, or sister they took a fancy. A story very similar to this is told in the Egil's Saga, and in the Eyrbyggia Saga Styrr, the son of Thorgrim, gets rid of two of these men by the most unscrupulous treachery. They were probably such a nuisance to society that anything was thought fair against them. The "Holmgang" was so called because the parties used often to fight in a "holm," or small island. Compare the preface to Mr. Dasent's Nial's Saga, and Maurer, Enstehung des Isländ. Staats, ss. 596, 599. See also the story which follows in chapter vi.

escort him to the field with a large number of men, so that the pirate might not seize on his property. He added that Asgaut had killed many of his people, and that he must give up his sister to him if they would not support him; "for," said he, "I have no confidence in the result of the 'holmgang,' unless I have the benefit of the good luck which attends you."

They did not like to refuse to go with him, and so they went into the upland with thirty men in their company; when they got to the place of meeting the question was put to all the people there, "Was there any man who desired to win a wife by fighting Asgaut?" but though the lady was attractive enough, there was no one ready to win her a that price. Then the brothers asked Eyiolf to bear Thorstein's shield for him in the fight, [1] but he replied that he never defended any other man, and not even himself in that way. "I shall not like it," said he, "if he is killed whilst he is under my care, and there could be no honour in that." "But if this young fellow is slain on our hands now, what are we to do? Are we to go away again when that is done, or are we to get a second and third man to fight the Berserker? Our disgrace will only increase in proportion as more men are killed on our side, and we shall get little credit by our journey if we go back without avenging him who thus falls, as it were, on our behalf." "Ask me, if you like, to fight the Berserker myself; that is a thing one may do for one's friends, but what you now ask I will not grant." They thanked him much, but the stake to be risked seemed very great in his case.

"Well," observed Eyiolf, "my opinion is, that none of our people ought to go back to their homes again, if the man who falls is not avenged, and I think it worse to fight the Berserker after

---

[1] That is to say to act as his second. See the story of Hermund, quoted by Maruer, from the Saga of Gunnlaug Ormstunga Enstehung des Isländischen Staats, s. 202.

your kinsman is killed than it would be before." So he stepped forward, and Ivar offered to hold the shield for him. Eyiolf answered-- "It is well offered, but the matter concerns me most, and the old proverb is true, a man's own hand is most to be trusted." Then he went on to the holm, and the Berserker called out, "Is that fellow going to fight with me?" "Is it not true," said Eyiolf, "that you are afraid to fight with me? It may be that you are not of the right sort when you fear a big man, and crow over a little one." "That has never been laid to my charge," replied the Berserker, "but I will explain to you the laws of the combat. If I am wounded I am to get off by paying five marks." "Oh," said Eyiolf, "I do not feel bound to keep any rules with you, when you set your own price on yourself, and that price is one which in our country would be paid for a thrall." Eyiolf had to strike the first blow, and that first blow he struck in such a way that if fell on the point of the Berserker's shield, and cut it off, and his foot along with it. He got great honour by this feat, and returned home with the brothers. A good deal of money was offered for his acceptance, but he said he had not done the deed for the sake of money, nor for the sake of the lady, but out of friendship for Hreidar and Ivar. Asgaut paid the fine to be released from the duel, and lived a maimed man.

After all this Eyiolf wooed Astrida, the daughter of Vigfuss, and the brothers went to press his suit for him. They said he was a man of great family, who held a good position in Iceland, and had many kinsmen to back him, and they thought it probable his career would be a distinguished one. Eyiolf himself then said, "It may be that Astrida's friends think we are boasting in what we say, but many know the fact of my having in Iceland an honourable descent and a good property." Vigfuss answered, "This will be her destiny, though we did not look lower for our kinswoman," and so she was betrothed to him and they sailed out to Iceland together.

# CHAPTER V.

THERE was a man named Bödvar; he was the son of Vikingakari, and the brother of Sigurd the father of Vigfuss, whose daughter was Astrida, the mother of Erik father of another Astrida, the mother of Olaf, the son of Tryggvi. Vikingakari was the son of Eymund the pirate, [1] the son of Thorir. Bödvar was the father of Oluf the mother of Gizor the white. When Eyiolf and his wife Astrida got out to Iceland, Ingiald was dead, and Eyiolf succeeded to his property and his office as priest. Ingiald had a daughter named Ulfeida, who was married to Narvi of Hrisey. Four children of Eyiolf and Astrida are mentioned, of whom Thorstein was the eldest, but his share of the inheritance was paid him when he married, and he dwelt on Eyjafirth as long as he lived, and has little to do with our story. The second was Vigfuss, who married Halfrida, the daughter of Thorkel the tall from Myvain. Glum was the youngest of their sons, and the daughter was named Helga. She was wedded to Steingrim of Sigluvik, and their son was Thorvald Tafalld, who comes up afterwards in this story. Vigfuss, however, died very soon after his marriage, leaving one child, who survived him a short time only, and thus it came to pass that all his property vested half in Halfrida and half in Glum and Astrida, for Eyiolf was dead before this happened. Then Thorkel the tall moved his establishment to Thverà, and Sigmund his son with him. The latter was a man of much importance, an looked

---

[1] The second name of Eymund, which I have translated "Pirate," may mean "the spoiler of ships," or the "spoiler of acres," according as it is written "Askaspillir," or Akraspillir." Myvatn, mentiond shortly afterwards, signifies "midge-water," or "gnat water."

forward to becoming chief of the district, if he made a good match, and got the support of good kinsmen.

Thorir was the name of a man who lived at Espihole, the son of Hamund of the dark-skin, and of Ingunna, the daughter of Helgi the thin. He had married Thordis, the daughter of Kadal, and their children were Thorarin and Thorvald the crooked, who lived at Grund on the Eyjafirth, Thorgrim, who lived at Mödrufell, Ingunna, the wife of Thord the priest of Frey, and Vigdis, who married Sigmund.

Now Thorkel and Sigmund took to disturbing the property of Astrida, [1] and they divided the land in half, but Glum and his mother got that part which had no house on it. So they made their dwelling at Borgarhole, but Glum took very little trouble about household matters, and seemed to be somewhat slow in coming to his full faculties. He was for the most part silent and undemonstrative, tall, of a dark complexion, [2] with straight white hair; a powerful man, who seemed rather awkward and shy, and never went to the places where men met together.

The temple of Frey was on the south of the river at Hripkelstad. Thorarin, of Espihole, was a prudent and popular man, but his brother Thorvald the crooked was a bully and hard to deal with. Sigmund thought he should be a great man if he could ally

---

[1] Thorkel and his son claimed, of course, as representing the interest of Halfrida, the widow of Vigfuss, Glum's brother. The other half of Vigfuss's property, after the death of himself and his child, returned to his mother and brother.

[2] The Icelandic word is "Skolbrunn," and its meaning is uncertain. If, as has been supposed, it had to do with the brow, it would probably be written "Skolbrynn." The senses given in the text is that suggested by my friend Mr. Vigfusson, the editor of the Eyrbyggia Saga (Leipzig, 1864.)

himself to the people at Espihole. In the meantime the property of Glum and Astrida was getting less every day, and their condition became uncomfortable, for Sigmund and Thorkel thwarted them, so that in everything they got less than their share. Then Glum says to his mother that he will go abroad, "for I see clearly I shall never get on here, but it may be I shall meet with more luck by means of the reputation of my kindred: I do not like to bear the encroachments of Sigmund, for whom as yet I am no match. However, do not you let go your hold on the land, through your position may be a difficult one." Glum at that time, when he desired to go abroad, was fifteen years of age.

# CHAPTER VI.

NOW we have to tell of Glum's voyage. As soon as he landed in Norway he went up to Vigfuss's house; and when he came thither he saw a great crowd of people, and all sorts of amusements and games going on. He understood at once that everything there must be on a great scale, but he saw many men of mark, and did not know which was his kinsman Vigfuss. He made him out by observing a tall and distinguished-looking man, in a full blue cloak, on the high seat, playing with a gold-mounted spear. Then Glum went up to him and greeted him, and his greeting was received courteously. Vigfuss asked who he was; he replied that he was an Icelander from Eyjafirth. Vigfuss inquired after his son-in-law, and his daughter Astrida. Glum told him that the former was dead, but that the latter was still living. Then he asked what children of theirs were alive, and Glum gave an account of his brothers and his sister, and added that he who now stood before him was one of the sons, but when he had said that, the conversation went no further. Glum asked Vigfuss to assign him a seat, but he said he did not know how much of what had been told him was true, told him to take a seat on the outside of the lower bench, and took little notice of him. Glum spoke little, and was unsociable in his habits, and when men were drinking or amusing themselves in other ways, he used to lie with his cloak wrapt round his head, so that he seemed a sort of fool. At the commencement of winter there was a feast prepared, and a sacrifice to the gods, in which observance all were expected to take part, but Glum sat in his place and did not attend it. As evening passed on, and the guests had arrived, there was not so much merriment, on account of the meeting of friends and the welcoming one another, as might have been expected when so many had come together. On the day on which the people came, Glum had not stirred out to meet them, nor did he ask any one to sit by him ort to take his place.

After they were set down to table, it was said that the man called "Biörn with the Iron Skull," and eleven others with him, were come into the homestead. He was a great Berserker, who used to go about to feasts where many people were assembled, and picked a quarrel with any one who chose to say anything which he could take hold of; the he challenged them to the "holmgang:" and Vigfuss therefore desired that every one should take care what he said. "For," said he, "it is less disgrace to do that than to get something worse at his hands." This all men promised to observe, and Biörn walked into the hall and looked for compliments, and asked the last man on the upper bench whether he thought himself as good a man as he (Biörn) was?" to which the reply was "Very far from it." Then he asked the same question of one man after the other, until he got up in front of the high seat. People used different words in answering him, but the end of it was that no one professed to be his match. When he came up to Vigfuss he asked him if he knew where to find such champions as he (Biörn) was? Vigfuss said he did not know any men equal to him. "Well," said Biörn, "that is a proper and discreet answer, as might have been expected from you, for you are an honourable man, and your life has been according to your wishes, without any check to your prosperity or any stain on your reputation. It is well therefore that I need address nothing but fair words to you, but I wish to ask you one question--Do you think yourself as good a man as I am?" Vigfuss replied, "When I was young, out sea-roving and getting some honour of my own--well, I do not know whether I might then have been your match, but now I am not half as good, for I am old and decrepid." Biörn turned away and proceeded further out along the second bench, and went on asking men whether they were his equals, but they all answered that they were not so. At last he came to the place where Glum lay stretched out on the bench. "Why does this fellow lie there," said Biörn, "and not sit up?" Glum's comrades answered for him and spoke on his behalf, and said that he was so dull that it mattered little what he said. Biörn gave him a kick, told him to sit up like other people, and asked him if he was as brave a man as he? Glum replied that Biörn had no need to meddle with him, and that he (Glum) knew nothing about his courage; "but there is one reason," he added, "why I should not like to be put on the same footing with you, and that is because out there, in Iceland, a man would be called a fool who conducted himself as you do, but here I see everybody regulates his speech in the most perfect manner." Then he jumps up, pulls Biörn's helmet off, catches up a stick of firewood, and brings it down between his shoulders, so that the great champion bends beneath the stroke. Glum gives him one blow after another till he is down, and then, as he tries to get on his feet, he smites him on the head, and so he goes on till he gets him outside the door. When Glum wanted to return to his seat, Vigfuss had come down from the dais to the floor of the hall and greeted his kinsman, telling him that he had now shown what he was, and proved that he belonged to the race. "Now I shall honour you as befits us," said Vigfuss; and he added that he acted as he had done at first, because Glum seemed slow and stupid. "I chose to wait till you on your way into our family by some act of manhood." Then he led him up to a seat next himself, and Glum told him he would have accepted that place before, if it had been offered to him. The next day they heard of Biörn's death, and Vigfuss offered Glum to succeed to himself in his position and dignity. The latter said he would accept the offer, but he must first go to Iceland in order to see that his inheritance there did not fall into the hands of those whom he did not choose should enjoy it, but that he would return as soon as possible. Vigfuss expressed his conviction that Glum would do credit to his race and increase his reputation in Iceland. So when summer came he got a ship ready for Glum, and put a cargo on board, with much store of gold and silver, and said to him, "I feel sure we shall not see one another again; but certain special gifts I will give you, that is to say, a cloak, a spear, and a sword, which we in this family have put great trust in. Whilst you retain these articles, I expect that you will never lose your honour; but if you part with them, then I have my fears:" and so they separated.

# CHAPTER VII.

GLUM sailed out to Iceland, and went home to Thverá, where he straightway found his mother. She received him gladly, and told him the unfairness of Sigmund and his father towards her. She bade him however have patience, for that she was not able to cope with them. Then he rode to the homestead, and saw that the fence ran in such a way as to encroach on his property, and he sung these verses:--

Yes! closer than I thought, fair dame,
This hedge so green hath hemm'd us in;
Our peace at home is spoilt, and shame
Must cling to us and all our kin.

I sing it now, but in the fray
I soon shall have to draw my sword.
Too surely, whilst I've been away,
My land hath found a wrongful lord.

What had occurred whilst he was absent, was that Sigmund had worried Astrida, and evidently wanted to drive her off her land. In the autumn, before Glum returned, Sigmund and Thorkel had lost two heifers, and supposed they had been stolen. Their suspicions fell on the serfs of Astrida, who, they said, had no doubt killed and eaten them off hand, and they caused these serfs to be summoned in the spring for the theft. Now these were the best men Astrida had, and she thought she could hardly mange her farm if they went away. So she went to her son Thorstein, and told him what wrong Sigmund and his father were doing her, and asked him to answer for her serfs. "I would rather atone for them in money," she said, "than that they should be found guilty on a false charge, and I should think it your business now to stand before us, and to show yourself worthy of a good name." Thorstein seemed to think that the prosecutors would so follow up the matter as to bring the full force of their family interest to bear on it. "And if," said he, "these serfs are essential to your household, we had better take such a share of the fine as will make it possible to get the money to pay it." "Yes," she answered, "but I hear that the only atonement they will take is one which is intended to ruin us. However, as I see there is a little help to be got where you are, the matter must rest in their hands."

One of the best things about the estate at Thverá was a certain field known by the name of "the Suregiver," which was never without a crop. It had been so arranged in the partition of the land that either party should have this field year and year about. Then Astrida said to Thorkel and Sigmund, "It is clear thay you wish to push me hard, and you see that I have no one to manage for me, but rather than give up my serfs I will leave the affair to be settled on your own terms." They replied that was very prudent on her part, and after consulting together they decided that they must either declare the men guilty, or award what damages they thought proper. But Thorstein did not stir in the case, so as to take the award out of their hands, and they assigned to the field to themselves, as sole owners, with the intention of getting hold of all her land, by thus depriving her of the main prop of her housekeeping. And that very summer which was coming on, she ought, if she had her rights, to have had the field.

Now, in the summer, when men were gone to the Thing, and when this suit had been thus settled, the herdsmen going round the pastures found the two heifers in a landslip, where the snow had drifted over them early in the winter, and thus the calumny against Astrida's serfs was exposed. When Thorkel and Sigmund heard that the heifers had bee found, they offered money to pay for the field, but they refused to renounce the conveyance which had been made of it to them. Astrida however answered that it would not be too great a compensation for the false charge which had been go up, if she were allowed to have what was her own. "So," said she, "I will either have what belongs to me, or I will submit to the loss; and though there is no one here to set the matter straight, I will wait, and I expect that Glum will come out and put it in the right way." Sigmund replied, "It will be a long time before he ploughs for that harvest. Why, there is that son of yours, who is a much fitter man to help you, sitting by and doing nothing." "Pride and wrong," said she, "often end badly, and this may happen in your case."

It was somewhat late in the summer when Glum came out; he stayed a little while with the ship, and then went home with his goods. His temper and character were the same as thy had been. He gave little sign of what he thought, and seemed as if he did not hear what had happened whilst he was away. He slept every day till nine o'clock, and took no thought about the management of the farm. If they had had their right, the field would, as had been said, have been that summer in the hands of Glum and his mother. Sigmund's cattle moreover did them much injury, and were to be found every morning in their home-field.

One morning Astrida waked Glum up, and told him that many of Sigmund's cattle had got into their home-field, and wanted to break in among the hay which was laid in heaps, "and I am not active enough to drive them out, and the men are all at work." He answered, "Well, you have not often asked me to work, and there shall be no offence in your doing so now." So he jumped up, took his horse, and a large stick in his hand, drove the cattle briskly off the farm, thrashing them well till they came to the homestead of Thorkel and Sigmund, and then he let them do what mischief they please. Thorkel was looking after the hay and the fences that morning, and Sigmund was with the labourers. The former called out to Glum, "You may be sure people will not stand this at your hands--that you should damage their beasts in this way, though you may have got some credit while you were abroad." Glum answered, "The beasts are not injured yet, but if they come again and trespass upon us some of them will be lamed, and you will have to make the best of it; it is all you will get; we are not going to suffer damage by your cattle any longer." Sigmund cried, out, "You talk big, Glum, but in our eyes you are now just as great a simpleton as when you went away, and we shall not regulate our affairs according to your nonsense." Glum went home, and then a fit of laughter came upon him, and affected him in such a manner that he turned quite pale, and tears burst from his eyes, just like large hailstones. He was often afterwards taken in this way when the appetite for killing some one came upon him.

# CHAPTER VIII.

WE are told that as the autumn went on Astrida came and spoke to Glum another morning, and, waking him up, asked him to give directions about the work, for the haymaking, she said, would be finished this day if all was ordered as it ought to be. Sigmund and Thorkel had already finished their hay, and they had gone early in the morning to the field "Sure-giver;' "and they are no doubt very well pleased in having that field, which we should have, if all were as it should be." Then Glum got up, but he was not ready before nine o'clock. He took his blue cloak, and his spear with gold about it in his hand, and got his horse saddled. But Astrida said to him, "You take a good deal of pains about your dress, my son, for haymaking." His answer was, "I do not often go out to labour, but I shall do a good stroke of work, and I will be well dressed for it. However, I am not able to give directions for the farm-work, and I shall ride up to Hole and accept the invitation of my brother Thorstein." So he crossed over to the south side of the river, and as he came to the field he took the brooch out of his cloak. Vigdis and her husband Sigmund were in the field, and when she saw Glum she came towards him and greeted him, saying, "We are sorry that our intercourse as relations is so little, and we wish in everything to do our part to increase it." Glum told her, "I have turned in here because the brooch is gone from my cloak, and I want you to put a stitch in it for me." She said she would do it with pleasure, and did it accordingly. Glum looked over the field and remarked, "Sure-giver has not yet lost his character." Then he put on his cloak again, took his spear in his hand, and turned sharp on Sigmund, with it uplifted. Sigmund sprang up to meet him, but Glum struck him on the head so that he needed no second blow. [1] Then he went up to Vigdis, and told her to go home, "and tell Thorkel, on Glum's part, nothing is yet done which will necessarily hinder our being on the footing of kinsmen, but that Sigmund is unable to leave the field." Glum rode on to Hole, and said nothing to his brother of what had happened; but when Thorstein saw how he was equipped, and how he had his cloak and spear, and perceived the blood in the ornaments of the weapon, [2] he asked him if he had used it within a short time. "Oh," cried Glum, "it is quite true; I forgot to mention it, I killed Sigmund, Thorkel's son, with it to-day." "That will be some news," replied Thorstein, "for Thorkel and his kinsmen at Espihole." "Yes," said glum; "however, as the old saying is, 'The nights of blood are the nights of most impatience.' No doubt they will think less of it as time goes on." He staid three nights at his brother's house, and then got ready to return home. Thorstein was preparing to ride with him, but Glum told him, "Look after your won household--I shall ride the straight path home to Thverá; they will not be so very keen in this business." So he went home to Thverá.

Thorkel went to see Thorarin, and asked him for counsel as to the course to be taken. His answer was, "It may now be that Astrida will say, Glum has not got on his legs for nothing." "Yes,"

---

[1] Glum's spear was probably a sort of halberd, with which he could either cut or thrust; such as is called "höggspiót," in Chapter xxii.

[2] The words of the text are that he saw the blood "I málunum," which may mean in "the marks--letters--or ornaments of the weapon." Runes or letters were sometimes engraved on the blade of a sword or spear. In the Edda, the sword which Sigurd lays on the bridal bed between himself and Brynhilda is called "mæki málfáinn," which is interpreted "ornamented" (Sigurdarkvida iii. stanz 4), and again a similar epithet is applied to the sword which Skirnir shows to Gerda (Skirnismál, stanza 23). In both cases it may mean "bearing runes or letters chased on the blade."

said Thorkel, "but I trow that he has got on that leg which will not bear him long." Thorarin replied, "That is as it may be. You have long dealt unfairly with them, and tried to turn them out, without considering what was to be expected from the descendants of one such as Eyiolf, a man of great family and withal himself of great courage. We are closely connected with Glum by kindred, and with you by marriage, and the suit seems a difficult one, if Glum follows it up, as I think he will." Thorkel then returned home, and the whole matter was kept quiet through the winter; but Glum had somewhat more men about him than he usually had.

# CHAPTER IX.

IT is said that Glum had a dream one night, in which he seemed to be standing out in front of his dwelling, looking towards the firth; and he thought he saw the form of a woman stalking up straight through the district from the sea towards Thverá. She was of such height and size that her shoulders touched the mountains on each side, and he seemed to go out of the homestead to meet her and asked her to come to his house; and then he woke up. This appeared very strange to every one, but he said, "The dream is no doubt a very remarkable one, and I interpret it thus--My grandfather, Vigfuss, must be dead, and that woman who was taller than the mountains, must be his guardian spirit, for he too was far beyond other men in honour and in most things, and his spirit must have been looking for a place of rest where I am." But in the summer, when the ships arrived, the news of Vigfuss's death became known, and then Glum sang as follows--

"At dead of night, beneath the sky,
Upon the banks of Eyjafirth,
I saw the spirit stalking by,
In giant stature o'er the earth.

"The goddess of the sword and spear
Stood, in my dream, upon this ground;
And whilst the valley shook with fear,
She tower'd above the mountains round."

In the spring Thorkel met Thorvald the crooked, and other sons of Thorir, and asked them to follow up this suit of his, referring to the tie which united them throurgh Thorir's daughter, and to all the friendship which he and his son Sigmund had shown to them. Thorvald spoke to Thorarin, and said that it would be discreditable to them not to help their brother-in-law, and he replied that he was ready to do all he could, and besides, he said, "It is now clear that Glum means to turn the slaying of Sigmund to account, so as to make himself a great man, and we think ourselves worth as much as he is in the district." "Yes," replied Thorarin, "but it seems to me it will be hard to follow up the suit, so as to make sure that we shall get any advantage by it, and on the other hand it is not unexpected that Glum should take after his race and kindred. I am slower to move in it than you are, because I doubt if any honour is to be got in a quarrel with Glum; yet I should not like to see our credit lowered." Hoever, after a certain pressure, Thorarin, the son of Thorir, set on foot at the Althing the suit against Glum for the slaying of Sigmund; and Glum set on foot a suit against Thorkel the tall, for slander against Astrida's serfs; and another against Sigmund, whom he charged with theft, and whom he alleged that he had killed while trespassing on his own property. So he summoned him as outlawed, inasmuch as he fell on his, Glum's, land, and he dug his body up. In this condition matters were when they went to the Althing. Then Glum visited his kinsmen, and sought for help at the hands of Gizor the white, and Teit, the son of Ketilbiörn of Mosfell, and Asgrim, the son of Ellidagrim; and he told them the whole course of the proceedings, and how Thorkel and Sigmund had encroached on his rights, and all the wrong and disgrace they had inflicted on him. But from them, he said, he expected help to put matters in a better condition. He himself would conduct the suit. They all professed themselves bound to take care that his cause was not left in unfriendly hands, and said they should be glad to see him distinguish himself among their kin.

The Thing went on till the court sat, and the men of Espihole preferred their suit for the slaying of Sigmund, rather as if they were egged on by those who had wrongs to revenge, than by those who felt sure that there were no flaws in their case. Glum too moved in the case against Thorkel, and the two suits came before the court. Glum had many kinsmen and friends to back him, and when, as defendant, he was called on to answer, he said, "The matter is on this wise. Every one may see that you have gone into this suit more as a question of temper than because there were no defects in your case, for I slew Sigmund trespassing on my own property, and before I rode to the Thing I proclaimed him as an outlaw." Then he named his witnesses on this point, and defended his suit with the help of his kinsmen, in such sort that judgment was given to the effect that Sigmund had been killed out of the pale of the law. Glum next took up the charge against Thorkel for trespass on his property, and the case looked ill for Thorkel, for the witnesses were on Glum's side, and there was no legal defence, so that it ended in seeking to compound the matter with the plaintiff. Glum said two courses were open--either he would follow the case out to its conclusion, or Thorkel must reconvey the land that Thverá at such a price as he should put on it, which was not more than half its worth. "And Thorkel may be sure," he added, "if he is convicted, that we shall not both of us be at the Thing next summer." The friends of Thorkel now interfered to get him to compound the suit, and he took the course which was expedient, settled the matter, and conveyed the land to Glum. He was to live on the land for the year, and thus, so to speak, they were on terms again. But the men of Espihole were ill pleased with the conclusion of these suits, and from that time they were never on a good footing with Glum. Indeed, before Thorkel left Thverá, he went to Frey's temple, and taking an old steer up thither, made this speech:--"Thou, Frey," said he, "wert long my protector, and many offerings hast thou had at my hands, which have borne good fruit to me. Now do I present this steer to thee, in the hope that Glum hereafter may be driven by force off this land, as I am driven off it; and, I pray thee, give me some token whether thou acceptest this offering or not." Then the steer was stricken in such a way that he bellowed loud and fell down dead, and Thorkel took this a a favourable omen. Afterwards he was in better spirits, as if he thought his offering was accepted and his wish ratified by the god. Then he removed to Myvatn, and we have doe with him in this story.

# CHAPTER X.

GLUM now assumed a high position in the district. There was a man named Gunnstein, who lived at Lón in Högardal, a great and rich man, reckoned to be one of the most important persons in the land. He had a wife called Hlif, and their son was Thorgrim, generally known as "Thorgrim the son of Hlif," being called after his mother because she outlived his father. She was a woman of a high spirit, and Thorgrim himself was all that a man ought to be, and became eminent. Another son of theirs was Grim, surnamed "Eyrar-leggr," and their daughter was Halldora, who was a beautiful woman of a gentle temper. She was esteemed to be about the best match in the country both on account of her kindred and of her own accomplishments and great qualities. Glum paid his addresses to her, stating that he did not want the help of kinsmen to explain what his family or his property and personal merits were. "All that you know well enough, and I have set my mind on this marriage is so be that it is agreeable to her friends." He received a favourable answer to his suit, and Halldora was betrothed to him with a great portion; so the wedding went of prosperously, and Glum's position became one of more dignity that it was before.

Thorvald was the son of Reim, who lived at Bard, in "the Fleets:" [1] he had to wife Thurida, the daughter of Thord of Höfdi. Their

---

[1] As a general rule I have not attempted to translate the proper names, but in this case and in that of "the Tarns" I have given the corresponding English appelations. The shallow pieces of water in the Essex marshes are still called "Fleets," and "Tarn" is well known in the north of England.

children were Klaufi and Thorgerda, whom Thorarin of Espihole had married. Thorvald the crooked of Grund wedded Thorkatla of Thiorsádal. Hlenni the Old, the son of Ornolf "Wallet-back," dwelt at Vidines, and he had to wife Otkatla, the daughter of Otkel of Thiorsádal. Gizor was the son of Kadal, and lived at "The Tarns," in the valley of Eyjafirth; his wife was named Saldis, and she was a worthy matron. Gizor was one of the most considerable landowners, well to do in respect of property, with two daughters, named Thordis and Herpruda, both handsome women, who were distinguished in dress and appearance and were considered good matches. They grew up to womanhood at home. Gizor's brother was called Runolf, and he was the father of Valgerda, mother of Eyiolf of Mödrufell. Thordis was Kadal's daughter, and she was married to Thorir of Espihole, and they had the children who have been named before. Thorgrim, however, the son of Thorir, although born in wedlock, was not the child of Thordis. He was a brave and well conditioned man, and he set out to meet Gizor and ask Thordis his daughter to wife for himself. His brothers and kinsmen too were engaged in pressing this suit. The maiden's relatives thought that they ought all to have a voice in the disposal of their kinswoman, and they all considered the proposal an excellent one; but notwithstanding this Thorgrim was refused. It seemed to pepole in general that Thorgrim had proposed a fair and equal match, and his brothers and kinsmen were offended at his rejection.

# CHAPTER XI.

WE must now bring into the story the man named Arnor, who was called "Red-cheek," the son of Steinolf, the son of Ingiald and first cousin of Glum. He had been long abroad, but was highly esteemed, and constantly with Glum when he was in Iceland. He suggested to Glum to get him a wife. Glum asked him what woman he wished to woo? He replied, "Thordis, the daughter of Gizor, who was refused to Thorgrim, the son of Thorir." "Well," said Glum, "that seems to me a hopeless proposal, for there is nothing to choose betwixt you two personally; but Thorgrim has a good establishment, plenty of money, and many kinsmen to back him, whereas you, on the other hand, have no household and not much property. I do not want to offer an unequal match to Gizor, so as to prevent him doing the best for his daughter, as he wishes, for Gizor deserves well at my hands." Arnor answered him, "I get the benefit of having good friends, if I make a better match in consequence of your urging my suit. Promise him your friendship, and then he will give me the girl. Indeed, it might have been called a fair match enough, if she had not been already refused to so good a man as Thorgrim." Glum allowed himself to be persuaded and went with Arnor to Gizor and pressed the matter on his behalf. Gizor's answer was, "It may be, Glum, that people will say I have made a mistake, if I give to Arnor, your kinsman, my daughter, whom I did not choose to give to Thorgrim." "Well," said Glum, "there is some reason in that; but it may also be said, if you will give proper weight to what I say, that my hearty friendship is to be thrown into the balance." Gizor replied, "Yes; but, on the other side, I suspect there will be the emnity of other people." "Well," said

Glum, "you see your way before you; but I tell you that what you do makes a great difference in my disposition towards you." Then said Gizor, "You shall not go away this time without succeeding;" so he gave him his and, and the girl was betrothed to Arnor. Glum insisted on one condition--that the bridal was to be at Thverá in the autumn; and they parted on this under-standing.

Now Arnor had some malt out at Gásar, and he himself and one of his men were to fetch it. [1] Thorgrim, son of Thorir, went to the warm spring on the very day on which they were expected in with the malt, and he was at the bath at Hrafnagil with six of his own men in his company. So when Arnor was coming up and wanted to cross the river, Thorgrim exclaimed, "Is not this a lucky hit, now, to stumble on Arnor? Do not let us miss the malt, at any rate, if we have missed the lady." They went at them with their swords uplifted, and Arnor, when he saw what the difference in their number was, jumped right into the river and got across; but his pack-horses remained on the west side of the stream. "Ah!" exclaimed Thorgrim, "we are not altogether out of luck; we shall drink the ale, if they get the wife." So he rode off to South Espihole. Thorir was then quite blind, and Thor-grim's companions were very merry and laughed aloud. Then Thorir asked what seemed so laughable to them. They said they did not know which party would have thier feast first; and they told him what they had got, and how the owners of the malt had been driven off, and how the bridegroom had jumped into the water. When Thorir heard the story he said, "Do you think you have made a good business of it now, that you laugh so heartily? How do you suppose you will get out of it? Do you imagine you will sleep quietly here to-night and want nothing

---

[1] Malt had to be imported into Iceland from Denmark or from England. See Laing, Heimskringla, i. p. 58. This malt apparently had been landed, and was waiting to be carried up the country.

else? Do you not know what Glum's disposition will be, if he approves of his kinsman's journey? I say it is good counsel to get our men together; it is most probable that Glum has already assembled a good many of his."

There was at that time a ford in the river at the place where now there is none. In the course of the night they collected some eighty good men, and stationed them on the edge of the rising ground, because the ford was just at that very point. On the other hand, it is to be told how Arnor found Glum and gave him an account of his expedition. "Yes," answered Glum, "this is pretty much what I expected; I did not think they would be quiet; and the matter is somewhat difficult to handle. If we do nothing there is disgrace for us, and the honour is not so clear if we try to set it right. However, we must get our men together." So when day broke Glum came to the river with sixty men and wanted to ride across, but the men of Espihole pelted them with stones, so that they did not advance; and Glum turned back whilst they fought with stones and missiles across the water. A good many men were wounded, but their names are not recorded. When the men of the district became aware of what was going on they came up in the course of the day and interfered, and the two parties came to a parley about terms. The men of Espihole were asked what satisfaction they would make for the insult offered to Arnor, and they said that no satisfaction was due from them, though Arnor had run away from his malt-sacks. Then a proposal was made that Glum should take part in asking, on behalf of Thorgrim, for Herpruda, the other daughter of Gizor, and that the marriage of Arnor and Thordis should take place only on condition of Glum's getting this second match agreed to. In fact, the one who was to be married to Thogrim was thought to have the best bargain. In consequence of the intervention of so many people, Glum promised his assistance in this matter, and he went to Gizor and spoke to him upon it. "It may seem," he said, "to be officious-ness on my part, if I take on myself to woo a wife for my own kinsman and for the men of Espihole too; but in order to stop disturbances in our district, I think I am bound to pledge my faith and friendship to you, if you will do as I wish." Gizpr replied, "It seems best to me that you should have you way, inasmuch as the offer to my daughter is a good one;" and so both matches were agreed on. Arnor went to live at Upsal, and Thorgrim at Mödrufell. Shortly after this Gizor died, and Saldis moved her household to Upsal. Arnor had a son by Thordis, who was called Steinolf, and Thorgrim had one who was named Arngrim, and was, as he grew up, a promising lad.

# CHAPTER XII.

SALDIS invited both her grandsons to stay with her. Arngrim was two winters older than Steinolf; there was not in the whole of the Eyjafirth any boys of a better disposition or greater promise, and they were very fond of each other. When one was four years old and the other six, they were one day playing together, and Steinolf asked Arngrim to lend him the little brass horse which he had. Arngrim answered, "I will give it you, for looking to my age, it is more fit for your plaything than mine." Steinolf went and told his foster-mother what a fair gift he had got, and she said it was quite right that they should be on such good terms with one another.

There was a woman who went about in that part of the country, named Oddbiörg, who amused people by story telling, and was a "spaewife." A feeling existed that it was of some consequence for the mistress of the house to receive her well, for that what she said depended more or less on how she was entertained. She came to Upsal, and Saldis asked her to spae something, and that something good, of those boys. Her answer was, "Hopeful are these lads; but what their future luck may be it is difficult for me to discern." Saldis exclaimed, "If I am to judge by this unsatisfactory speech of yours, I suppose you are not pleased with your treatment here." "You must not," said Oddbiörg, "let this affect your hospitality, nor need you be so particular about a word of this kind." "The less you say the better," replied Saldis, "if you can tell us nothing good." "I have not yet said too much," she answered; "but I do not think this love of theirs will last long." Then Saldis said, "I should have thought my good treatment of you deserved some other omen; and if you deal with evil bodings, you will have a chance of being turned out of doors." "Well," said Oddbiörg, "since you are so angry about nothing, I see no need for sparing you, and I shall never trouble you again. But, take it as you will, I can tell you that these boys will hereafter be the death each of the other, and one mischief worse than another for this district will spring from them." So Oddbiörg is out of our story.

# CHAPTER XIII.

IT happened one summer, at the Althing, that the Northern men and those of the West-firths met one another on the wrestling ground in a match according to their districts. The Northerners had rather the worst of it, and their leader was Márr, the son of Glum. Now a certain man of the name of Ingolf, the son of Thorvald, came up, whose father lived at Rangavellir. Márr addressed him thus--"You are a strong-limbed fellow, and ought to be sturdy; do me the favour of going into the match and taking hold." his answer was--"I will do so for your sake," and forthwith the man he grappled with went down, and thus it was with the second, and the third, so that the Northerners were well pleased. Then said Márr, "If you want a good word on my part, I shall be ready to help you. What may be your plans?" "I have no plans," he answered, "but I had an inclination to go northward and get work." "Well," rejoined Márr, "I should like you to go with me; I will get you a place." Ingolf had a good horse of his own, which he called b the name of "Snækoll," and he went northward to Thverá, after the Thing was over, and staid there some time. Márr asked him one day what he intended to do. "There is and over-looker wanted here, who ought to be somewhat handy; for instance, here is this sledge to be finished, and if you can do that you can do something worth having." "I should be too glad of such a place," said Ingolf, "but it has sometimes happened that my horses have caused trouble in the pastures of the cattle." "No one will talk about that here," answered Márr; so Ingiolf set to work on the sledge. Glum came up, and looked at what he was doing. "That is a good piece of work," he observed. "What are your plans?" Ingolf answered, "I have no plans." Glum replied, "I want an over-looker, are you used to that sort of business?" "Not much, in such a place as this, but I should be glad to stay with you." "Why should it not be so?" said Glum; "for I see that you and Márr get on well together." When Márr came home Ingolf told him what had passed. "I should like it much," he answered, "if it turns out well, and I will take care, if anything displeases my father, to tell you of it three times; but if you do not set it right then I must stop." So Ingolf took to his business, and Glum was pleased with him.

One day Glum and Ingolf, his over-looker, went to a horse-fight; the latter rode a mare, but the horse ran along by their side. The sport was good; Kálf, of Stockahlad was there, and he had an old working horse who beat all the others. He called out, "why don't they bring into the ring that fine-jawed beast of the Thverá people?" "They are no fair match," said Glum, "your cart-horse and that stallion." "Ah!" exclaimed Kálf, "the real reason why you will not fight him is because he has no spirit in him. It may be the old proverb is proved true, 'the cattle are like their master.'" "You know nothing about that," answered Glum, "and I will not refuse on Ingolf's part, but the fight must not go on longer than he chooses." "He will probably know well enough, said Kálf, "that little will be done against your wishes," The two horses were led out, and fought well, and all thought Ingolf's horse had the best of it; Glum then chose to separate them, and they rode home. Ingolf remained that year in his place, and Glum was well satisfied with him.

Not long after this there was a meeting at Diupadal, whither Glum, and Ingolf with his horse, came; Kálf also was there. This last man was a friend of the people of Espihole, and he demanded that they should now let the horses fight it out. Glum said it depended on Ingolf, but that he himself was against it; howerer, he did not like to back out of it, and the horses were led out accordingly. Kálf spurred his horse on, but Ingolf's horse had the best of it in every contest. Then Kálf struck Ingolf's horse over the ears with his staff in such a way as to make him giddy, but immediately afterwards he went at his adversary again. Glum came up, and fair fighting was restore, till in the end Kálf's horse bolted from the ring. Then there wars a great shout, and at last Kálf smote Ingolf with his stick. People interfered, and Glum said, "Let us take no note of such a matter as this; this is the end of every horse-fight." Márr, on the other hand, said to Ingolf, "Depend upon it, my father does not intend that any disgrace shall attach to you for this blow."

# CHAPTER XIV.

THERE was a man named Thorkel, who lived at Hamar. Ingolf went thither, and met this man's daughter, who was a handsome woman. Her father was well enough off, but he was not a person of much consideration in the country. Ingolf, however, attended properly to his duties as over-looker, but he did not work as a craftsman so much as he had done, and Márr spoke to him once about it saying, "I see that my father is not pleased at your being often away from home." Ingolf gave a fair answer, but it came to the same thing again, and Márr warned him again a second and third time, but it was no use.

One evening it happened that he came home late, and when the men had had their supper Glum said, "Now let us amuse ourselves, and let each of us say what or whom he most relies on, and I will have first choice. Well, I choose three things on which I most rely; the first is my purse, the second is my axe, and the third is my larder." Then one man after another made his choice, and Glum called out, "whom do you chose, Ingolf?" His answer was, "Thorkel, of Hamar." Glum jumped up, held up a the hilt of his sword, and going up to him said, "A pretty sort of patron you have chosen." All men saw that Glum was wroth. He went out, and Ingolf went with him, and then Glum said to him, "Go now to your patron and tell him you have killed Kálf." "Why," replied he, "how can I tell him this lie?" "You shall do as I please," answered Glum, so they both went together, and Glum turned into the barn, where he saw a calf before him. "Cut it's head off," he cried, "and then go southward across the river and tell Thorkel that you look to him alone for protection, and show him your bloody sword as the token of the deed you have done." Ingolf did this; went to Thorkel, and told him as news how he had not forgooten the blow Kálf had given him, and how he had killed him. The answer was, "You are a fool, and you have killed a good man; get you gone as quick as you can, I do not choose that you should be slain on my premises." Then Ingolf came back again to meet Glum, who asked him "Well, how did your patron turn out?" "Not over well," said he. "You will have trouble on your hands," remarked Glum, "if Kálf, of Stockahlad should really be killed."

Now Glum himself had killed Kálf, at Stöckahlad, whilst Ingolf was away, and had thus taken vengeance for him, [1] and the following day Kálf's death was publicly known. Thorkel said at once that a fellow had come thither who had taken the death on himself, so that everybody thought it was really so. The winter passed on, and Glum sent Ingolf northward, to the house of Einar, the son of Konál, and gave him nine hundred ells of cloth. "You have had no wages," he said, "from me," but with your saving habits you may turn this to good account, and as regards this matter which is laid to your charge I will take care of that. It shall not hurt you; I paid you off for your perverseness in this way, and when you come home you may come and pay me a visit." Ingolf answered, "One thing I beg of you, do not let the woman be married to any one else." "This, I promise you," said Glum. Ingolf's horses were left where they were. Einar, the son of Konál, got Ingolf conveyed abroad, but Thorvald began a

---

[1] This sentence appears to be as sort of gloss introduced in one of the transcripts from the original MS, but I have inserted it in the text, as it is essential to the understanding of this strange story. It should be observed that there is a double pun in the Icelandic which cannot be represented in a translation. Not only was the man's name Kálf, but he lived at Stocka-Hlad, and the calf which Ingolf was made to kill was in the hlada, or barn.

suit at the Hegranes Thing for the slaughter of Kálf, and it looked as if Ingolf would be found guilty. Glum was at the Thing, and some of Ingolf's kinsmen came to him, and asked him to look after the case, professing their readiness to contribute to pay the fine for him. Glum told them, "I will see to the suit without any fine being paid."

When the court went out to sit, and the defendant was called on for his defence, Glum stated that the suit was null and void, "for you have proceeded against the wrong man; I did the deed." Then he named his witnesses, who were to certify that the suit was void; "for though Ingolf did kill the 'calf' in the barn, I did not make any charge against him for that. Now, I will offer an atonement more according to the worth of the man killed, ant according to the pride of you men of Espihole." So he did, and the people left the Thing.

Ingolf was abroad that winter, and could stand it no longer, but turned his cash into goods, and purchased valuable articles, and tapestry hangings of rare quality. Glum had given him a good cloak, and he exchanged that for a scarlet kirtle. The summer that he had sailed there came out to Iceland the man called Thiodolf, whose mother lived at Æsustad. He visited Hamar, and fell in with Helga. One day Glum was riding up to Hole, and a he went down the hill at Saurbæ, Thiodolf met him. Glum said to him, "I do not like your visits to Hamar; I mean myself to provide for Helga's marriage, and if you do not give this up I shall challenge you to the 'Holmgang.'" He answered that he was not going to math himself with Glum, and so he left off going thither.

# CHAPTER XV.

THEN Ingolf came out to Iceland and went to Thverá, and asked Glum to take him in, which was granted. One day he said, "Now, Glum, I should like you to look over my merchandize." So he did, and it seemed to him that Ingolf had laid out his money well. Then Ingolf said, "You gave me the capital for this voyage, and I consider all the goods as belonging to you." "No," answered Glum, "what you have got is not enough for me to take anything from you." "Here," answered Ingolf, "are some hangings which I purchased for you--these you shall accept; and here is a kirtle." "I will accept your gifts," replied Glum.

Another time Glum asked him if he wished to remain at home with him, and Ingolf answered that his intention was not to part from him if he had the choice o staying. "My stud-horses I will give you," he said, and Glum replied, "The horses I will accept, and now to-day we will go and find Thorkel, at Hamar." Thorkel received Glum well, and the latter said, "You have wronged Ingolf, and now you must make it up to him by giving him your daughter in marriage--he is a proper man for this match. I will lay down some money for him, and I have proved him to be a worthy fellow. If you do not act thus, you will see that you have made a bad business of it." So Thorkel consented, and Ingolf got his wife and settled down as a householder and a good useful man.

# CHAPTER XVI.

GLUM married his daughter Thorlauga to Vigu-Skuta, of Myvatn, in the north country, but on account of disagreement the husband caused her to return to Thverà, and divorced her, which annoyed Glum much. Afterwards Arnor Kerlingarnef wooed her and had her to wife, and good men are sprung from that marriage. From this time there was a great feud between Glum and Skuta. One summer it happened that a vagabond fellow came to Skuta and asked to be taken in. He inquired what he had been doing, and the answered was that he had slain a man and could not stay in the district to which he belonged. Skuta replied, "Well, what are you ready to do to earn my protection?" "What do you ask for?" said the other. "Why, you shall go, as sent from me, to Glum's house, and tell him that you want him to take charge of your affair. I think it will turn out with reference to your meeting that he is now on his way to the Thing. He is a good man to help any one in trouble, if people want his aid; and it may be that he will tell you to go to Thverà and wait for him there. You will then say that you are in too great a strait for this, and that you would rather have some talk with him alone, and it may be that he will tell you what to do. An any rate ask him to let you meet in the Midárdal, which runs up from the homestead at Thverà and in which his pasture-huts stand; say that you would be glad to find him there on some day named for the purpose." The man assented to all this, and it was arranged as Skuta had proposed. Now this fellow, who was to serve as a bait, came back to Skuta and told him the whole. "You have done your work well," said he, "and you had better stay with me." Time passed on until the day came when Glum had promised the meeting, and then

Skuta gets ready to start from home with thirty men. He rides southward, and then west, over the heath of Vadla, and so on to the bank which is called "Red-bank," and there they dismount. Then Skuta says to his men, "You will have to stay here a little while, and I will ride further into the valley, along the side of the hill, to see if there is anything to be got." When he looks along the valley he sees a tall man, in a green cloak, riding up from Thverà, whom he knows to be Glum, and gets off his horse. He has a cape on him of two colours, one side black and the other white, and he leaves his horse in the clearing and goes up to the pasture-hut into which Glum has entered. Skuta holds in his hand the sword named "Fluga," with a helmet on his head; he goes up to the door, knocks upon the wall, and then steps on one side close to the hut. Glum comes out, without any weapon in his hand, and sees no one by the hut, but Skuta rushes forward between Glum and the doorway. Then Glum knows his man, and starts away from him. The gorge in which the river runs is near the hut. Skuta calls to him to wait, but he says it would be all right if they were armed in the same way, and makes for the gorge with Skuta after him. Glum jumps right into the gorge, but Skuta looks about to see where he can get down. Then he sees in the gorge a cloak driven along in the water, and runs towards it, thrusting at it with his sword; but he hears a voice calling out above him, "There is little honour to be won by spoiling people's clothes." He looks up and recognizes Glum; who in fact knew that there was a grassy bank on the edge of the stream where he jumped down. "Well," says Skuta, "remember one thing, Glum, you have run for it, and would not wait for Skuta." Glum's answer is, "That is true enough, and I only wish that, before sunset this day, you may have to run for it as far as I have done." Glum sung a verse--

"South of the river here, I trow,
Each bush is worth a crown;

Elsewhere the forest often saves
The outlaw hunted down." [1]

So they parted at that time; but Glum went home, got his people together, told them what a trap had been set for him, and expressed his desire to take vengeance for it at once. In a short time he collected sixty men and rode up into the valley. Skuta, after parting with Glum, got back to his horse, and riding along the hill-side he saw the men on their way. He thought it would not be good for him to meet them, so he made his plan, broke his spear-head off its shaft, handled this as if it were a pole, unsaddled his horse and rode bareback, with his cape turnd inside out, shouting as if he were looking for sheep. Glum's men overtook him and inquired if he had seen any man fully armed riding over the hill? He replied that he had seen one. "What is your name?" they asked. "I am called," he says, " 'Plenty' in the Myvatn country, but at Fiskelæk people call me 'Scarce.'" They answered, "You are making sport of us;" but he said he could not tell them anything truer than what he had told them, and so he parted from them. As soon as this was done he took up his daddle again and rode sharply off to his own men. Glum's people came up to him and told him they had met a man who had answered them with a jest, and they said what his name was. "You have made a blunder," said Glum; "it was Skuta himself that you fell in with. What could he say that was more true? In the Myvatn country caves (Skuta) are 'plenty,' and in Fiskelæk they are 'scarce.' He has come pretty close to us, and we must ride after him." So they came up to the bank where Skuta and his men were, but there was only one path up to it,

---

[1] I confess that I do not clearly understand the meaning of this stanza, unless Glum intends to say that any device was justifiable in getting away from Skuta in a country which offered such scanty means of escape. It may mean, however, that Skuta himself would have hard work to get away.

and the position was easier to defend with thirty men that it was to attack with sixty. Skuta then called out, "You have taken a good deal of trouble to follow me up, and I suppose you think you haves something to pay me for on account of your escape. No doubt you showed great presence of mind in jumping into the gorge, and you were pretty quick of foot about it." "Yes," said Glum, "and you had some reason to be afraid when you pretended to be a sheperd belonging to the Eyjafirth people, and hid your arms or broke some of them. I fancy you had to run quite as far as I did." Skuta replied, "However things may have gone up this time, try now to attack us with double our number." Glum's answer was, "I think we will part this time, whatever people may say of either of us." So Skuta rode away north, and Glum went home to Thverà.

# CHAPTER XVII.

WHEN Thorir died his son Thorarin set up his household to the north of Espihole and lived there. Glum had two children by his wife, of whom one was Márr, as has been said above, and the other was Vigfuss; both promising, but utterly unlike each other. Márr was quiet and silent, but Vigfuss was a dashing fellow, ready to do an unfair thing, strong and full of courage. There was a man living with Glum, who was called Hallvard, and was a freedman of his; he had brought Vigfuss up, and having got a good deal of property together by cheating in money matters , he had made over the reversion if it to his foster-child. Hallvard had a bad name, and went to live at a place called "The Tarns," in the valley of the Eyjafirth: nor did his reputation impove on account of the spot where he dwelt, for he was sharp in dealing with the cattle in the common pastures up there. Vigfuss was a great traveller

A man hight Halli lived at Jorunnarstad, who was called "Halli the white," and he was the son of Thorbiörn, whilst his mother was Vigdis, the daughter of Andun the bald. Now Halli had fostered Einar, the son of Eyiolf, who then lived at Saurbæ. Halli was blind, and was mixed up in all the lawsuits in the country because he was both a wise man and sound in his judgment. His sons were Orm and Brusi the Skald, who lived at Törfufell, and Bárd, who lived at Skállstad. Bárd was a noisy, quarrelsome fellow, better able to fight than anybody, and reckless and abusive in his language; he had for a wife Una, the daughter of Oddkell, in Thiorsádal.

One autumn Halli missed some ten or twelve wethers out of the hill pastures, and they could not be found, so when Bárd and his father met, Halli asked his son what he thought had become of the wethers. Bárd replied, "I don't wonder if sheep disappear, when a thief lives next door to you, ever since Hallvard came into the district. "Yes," says Halli, "I should like you to set on foot a suit against him, and summon him for theft. I don't think, if I make this charge against him, Glum will go the lengths of clearing him by the oath of twelve men." "No," answered Bárd, "it will be a difficult matter for him to get the oath of twelve men out of Glum and Vigfuss and their people." [1]

---

[1] See the Supplementary Note at the end of the book.

# CHAPTER XVIII.

THEN Bárd set his suit on foot, and when Vigfuss knew it, he told his father that he should not like proceedings for a theft to be commenced against his foster-father. Glum's answer was, "You know he is not to be trusted, and it will not be a popular thing to swear him guiltless." Vigfuss said, "Then I would rather that we had to deal with a matter of greater consequence." Glum replied, "It seems to me better to pay something on his account and let him change his residence and come hither, than to risk my credit for a man of his character."

When men came up to the Thing, the case was brought on in court, and Glum had to swear one way or the other with his twelve men. Vigfuss became aware of the fact that his father intended to find Hallvard guilty, so he went to the court and said that he would take care Glum should pay dearly for it, if his foster-father was declared guilty. It ended in Glum quashing the suit by swearing that Hallvard was innocent, and he got discredit by doing so. In the course of a winter or two it happened that Halli lost a pig of his, which was so fat that it could hardly get on its legs. Bárd came in one day and asked if he pig had been killed, and Halli said it had disappeared. Bárd replied, "he is gone, no doubt, to look for the sheep which were stolen last autumn." "I suppose," said Halli, "they are both gone the same way. Will you summon Hallvard?" "Well," replied Bárd, "so it shall be, for I do not think Glum will this time swear Hallvard free; Vigfuss was the cause of he previous acquittal, and he is not now in the country." Bárd took up the case and proceeded to serve the summons; but when he met Hallvard he made a short matter of the suit by cutting of his head, and went and told his father. Halli did not like it; he straightway found Glum, told him what had happened, and offered to leave the matter in his hands. Glum accepted the offer, assessed the damage at a small sum, and caused the pig and the sheep to be paid for, by doing which he was well spoken of. When Vigfuss returned he was displeased at Hallvard's death; but his father said, "I shall not allow this settlement to be disturbed now it is made;" and when Vigfuss and Bárd met nothing passed between them.

The next summer there was a meeting appointed for a horse-fight, in which all the horses in that district were to be fought; those from the upper against those from the lower "rape," [1] and either party were to select their man as umpire to decide which had the best of it. The judgment of the men thus chosen was to be abided by. From the upper "rape" Bárd was taken, and from the lower Vigfuss, the son of Glum. There were many horses, and the sport was good, but the fight was pretty equal, and many matches came off, with the result however that the number of those which fought well, and those which bolted was the same. so they agreed that it was an equal match; but Vigfuss said he had a horse which had not fought, which was the best on the ground that day. "Come," said he, "do you match some one with him." Bárd answered, "He looks a poor beast to us, we will not match any horse with him; let us say it is a tie." "Oh," replied Vigfuss, "the fact is you have none to meet him, but you do not choose to own that you have got the worst of it." "Up to this time," said Bárd, "You have acted impartially, but now the sky is clouding over. Now we see the truth, that you have stood by your mother at the dresser in the pantry, and talked about cooking oftener than you have been at horse-

---

[1] The Icelandic word is Hreppr--and I have translated it by the word still retained in "The Rape of Bramber."

fights, and that is the reason why your beard has never got any colour in it." Vigfuss and other people laughed at this joke.

Halli's servant came home, and his mater asked him about the horse-fights. He said the match was held to be "a tie." Then Halli asked, "Did Bárd and Vigfuss agree?" "Yes, pretty well, but Bárd said one thing to Vigfuss." "What was that?" he inquired; then the servant repeated it, and Halli said, "That will lead to mischief." The servant said, "Vigfuss laughed at it." "Yes, but it is the way of Glum and his son to laugh when the fit for killing somebody comes upon them."

When Halli and Bárd met, the former asked his son, "How came you to talk in that reckless way? I fear it will lead to great evil. You have but one thing to do, and that is to go abroad and get house timber; you must stay away three winters or your death is certain." Bárd answered, "There is nothing in it if you were not a coward, but old age causes you to be afraid on account of your sons." "You are no doubt a very brave fellow," said Halli, "but you will find it difficult to stay in the district." So Bárd took his father's advice and went abroad, and Halli bribed a vagrant fellow to go into Skagafirth, or to the westward of it, and tell the story how Bárd was gone away; and how for the sake of one word, on account of Glum and his son, the only safe course for him had been to become an exile; and ho no one in the district dared to do anything which they disliked. This fellow did what Halli wished, and they had recourse to this plan in order that Bárd's kinsmen might not be molested for his sake. Bárd stopped out one winter, and then returned to his home.

# CHAPTER XIX.

WHILST Bárd was away Halli took care of his property, and got some timber cut in a wood in Midárdal which belonged to him, and Bárd brought out a good deal of timber with him. Sometimes he stayed at his own home, and sometimes with his father. Bárd said he would go and fetch his timber home, when Halli remarked, "I would not have you go yourself, for it is not good to trust that father and son." "Oh," said Bárd, "nobody will know that I am going." So he went, and a servant with him, to fetch the timber, and they took a good many horses with them, but his wife Una had gone to Vidines to see her sister Oddkatla, and Bárd went thither on his way. Hlenni begged him to send some one else into the wood, and to stay where he was himself; it seemed more prudent to do so, but Bárd answered there was no need of it.

The two sisters went with him out of the homestead, but when they were returning Una looked back at him over her shoulder, and fell down in a swoon. Her sister asked her what she had seen? "I saw dead men coming to meet Bárd," said she; "he must be fey. We shall never see one another again." Bárd and his men made their way into the wood, and when they were there, they got their loads of timber together, and tied up their horses, but a great mist had come on. Very early that morning the shepherd from Thverà had been a-foot, and Vigfuss met him and asked him for tidings, as he often did. "It is wonderful to me," he said, "that you never fail to find your sheep in such a fog as there is now." The shepherd answered, "It is a small matter for me to find my flock, but those men whom I saw in the wood in the morning had more trouble to find their horses, which were really standing close to them. They were fine looking fellows; one was in a green kirtle, and they had shields by their sides." Vigfuss asked him if he knew the man? He said he thought it was Bárd, for he was the owner of the wood where they were. "Get my three horses," said Vigfuss. There were two Easterlings staying there whom Vigfuss asked to ride with him, saying that he was going to the warm spring; but when he got out of the homestead he made as if he would ride southward over Laugardal. The Easterlings asked him, "Whither are you riding now?" "On some business of my own first," said he, so he rode a good way in front of them, and they went southward above the enclosures, until they saw Bárd coming out of the wood with his loaded horses. Bárd's servant saw some one riding after them, and remarked, "These men are riding sharp after us." "Who is that?" said Bárd. "It is Vigfuss," he replied, "and I think we had better get away from him. There is no disgrace in doing so, whilst we know nothing of their intentions." Bárd said, "He will not set on me with three men, if you are not with me." "I would sooner go with the horses," answered the man, "and do you ride to Vidines. You cannot be blamed for going where you have business, and you do not know for a certainty what they who are riding after us want, thought Hlenni told you not to trust them." Bárd told him then, "You shall ride on forward and, if I am delayed, tell our men what is going on, for it is likely that I and Vigfuss shall be some time about it, if we look one another fairly in the face; and he is too good a man to set on me with three against one. If, on the other hand, we are two and they are three, they will take the benefit of the difference in strength."

The servant did what Bárd told him, and Bárd himself un-strapped his shield, and got ready in the best way he could. When they came up he asked what they wanted? Vigfuss said that both of them would not quit the meeting-place alive. Bárd replied that he was ready, if they two only were to play the game out; "but there is no manhood in it if three are to set on one." The Easterlings then said they would have staid at home if they had known their errand, but that they could not take part unless, in consequence of Bárds companion having ridden off, men should come to his assistance. Vigfuss told them to see first how matters went. So he and Bárd fought for some time without either being wounded, but it looked worse for Vigfuss, inasmuch as he had to give ground every time without being able to make a single blow tell. Bárd had his sword, and defended himself admirable without being touched. In the mean time the Easterlings thought it would be a bad business if Vigfuss should be slain, while they stood by doing nothing, and if men should come up to help Bárd. They they rushed at him, so that he was dying when Hlenni and his men got there. Vigfuss and his friends rode home, but Glum was ill pleased with what they had done, and said that the difficulties in the district would be greatly increased. Halli went to his foster-son Einar, at Saurbæ, and asked him to take the case in hand, and he admitted that he was bound to avenge his kinsman and foster-brother. Then they rode to Thorarin, and asked for his support; he replied that he knew no man he would rather have to deal with than Vigfuss, and they confirmed with oaths their alliance with reference to that and all other matters. The cause went to the Thing, and attempts were made to compound it, but there was so much in the way that it was difficult to effect a compromise, as both the men of Mödrufell and those of Espihole, who resisted it, were bold in spirit, and well versed in the law. The case was closed by a verdict against the Easterlings, and by money being given to allow Vigfuss a safe conduct. He was to have three summers to get a passage out, and to have three places of refuge in each year, but he was an outlaw on peril of his life elsewhere, and not allowed to be at home on account of the sacredness of the place. However, he stayed long at Upsal, though people thought he was in other quarters of the island,

and he would not go abroad within the period fixed. Then he became completely outlawed, and Glum kept him concealed, but outlawed men were not allowed to live there because Frey, who owned the temple, did not permit it. So matters went on for six winters.

# CHAPTER XX.

WE must now go back to the point where the foster-brothers Arngrim and Steinolf were growing up together. When Thorgrim of Mödrufell died, Arngrim went to his own house, and Steinolf remained with him, and there was as much affection between them as there had ever been. Arngrim took a wife, Thordis, the daughter of Biörn, and the sister of Arnor Kerlingarnef. Steinolf was at that time abroad, engaged in trading voyages, but when he was in Iceland he was at Arngrim's house. It happened one summer, on his arrival in the Eyjafirth, that Arngrim did not invite him to his house, and though they met he did not speak to him, imputing to him that he had talked with his wife, Thordis, more than was proper; but the report of most men was that there was little or nothing in the matter. Then Glum asked Steinolf to visit him, and he was there for a year or two when he was in Iceland, and they regarded one another with much affection as kinsmen. Steinolf was an active merry fellow. One summer Glum did not ask him to his house, and said that he preferred that he should be with his father at Upsal, "and my reason is, I do not approve of men living in other people's house, but if you are with your father then you can come over hither to Thverà, and I shall be glad to see you." Vigfuss, for some winters, whilst he was an outlaw, was at Upsal with Arnor Red-cheek, and Steinolf was there also. One autumn a yeoman at Öxnafell married his daughter, and invited all those land-owners in Eyjafirth, who were of most consequence; Steinolf too was invited. He came over to Thverà, and wanted to go with Glum, bout Glum said he should not be at the wedding. Then Steinolf observed, "What I do not like is that you do not abide by what you say." "Well," said Glum, "my want of consistency will not do so much harm as your want of prudence, and I will not go. It is a piece of presumption at any rate, if there is no deeper design in it, for a yeoman to ask so many men of consequence to his house. But I suspect that something more is meant that appears, and that the yeoman did not get up this scheme himself, so I think it better that I and my friends should stay away." Steinolf, however, and those who were asked, with the exception of Glum, went to the wedding. Einar, the son of Eyiolf, Thorvald, and Steingrim had a good deal of talk together. When people were going away, Einar made a long speech about the manage-ment of affairs in the district, and said it was fitting that when they met in any number they should talk over the matters of most urgency; that in this way things would get into a better state. "For instance," he said, "there has long been a bad feeling among men of the highest spirit, and I allude particularly to the fact that there is a quarrel between the two kinsmen Arngrim and Steinolf, whilst we think that some lie or calumny is at the bottom of it all. Now Arngrim wishes to invite Steinolf to his house, and will receive him honourably if he choose to accept the invitation. So get rid of all unfriendly feeling between you." Steinolf professed his readiness to accept the offer, and his unconsciousness of any cause of offence, and he added that he loved Arngrim above all men. The each man returned to his home, and Steinolf went back with Arngrim, and remained with him, for several nights with all honour.

# CHAPTER XXI.

ONE day Arngrim asked Steinolf if he would go down with him to Grund to a club-feast, and stay two or three nights. He replied, "I will stay at home now and go some other time when you are here." Arngrim expressed a hope that he would wait for his return, if he would not accompany him, and he went on to Grund, but Steinolf stayed over the night. In the morning Steinolf was sitting by the fire, with some work in hand; it was a certain casket which belonged to the lady of the house. At that moment Arngrim returned home with Thorvald the crooked, and as they came into the sitting-room Steinolf was bending down over his work. Then Arngrim struck him on the head in such a way as to cause his death; but the mistress of the house came up to him and exclaimed, "Wretch that thou are to strike this blow! This is the work of wiser men than thou art; but from this day I will never be they wife." She went to the house of Arnor Kerlingarnef and never came together with Arngrim again; but before she rode off she said, "It will be some consolation, Arngrim, that your days are to be few, for those which are to come will be worse for you." Afterwards she became the wife of Asgrim, Ellidagrim's son.

Arngrim and Thorvald rode to Espihole and told Thorarin what had happened, asking for his protection, and adding that whilst they had neither the wisdom nor the popularity to hold their own against Glum, he (Thorarin) had abundance of both. He replied to them and said that the deed seemed to be bad, and one from which apprehended evil consequences. Thorvald thought it was no use to find fault with what had been done, and that if he did not support them, he would soon have greater difficulties on his hands. They hoped to get other people to help them, if he would speak on their behalf. "My counsel," says Thorarin, "is that you should both remove from Grund and Mödrufell, and that we should collect men as soon as we may, and join our households together, before Glum is informed of it." They did this before Glum heard what had occurred; but when he learnt it he assembled his people, who proceeded to attack them. However, there was no opportunity for doing so with effect, as the men of Espihole had the larger force, and so they remained quiet for the winter. Glum, on the other hand, was never to be got at; he was so cautious about himself that he never slept in the bed which had been prepared for him. Very often he rested little at night, but he and Márr walked up and down and talked about lawsuits. One night Márr asked him how he had slept, and Glum answered by a stanza--

" 'Mid all this strife and tumult now
Sleep doth mine eyelids flee.
These men will find it hard, I trow,
To make their peace with me,

Before upon their crests shall ring
My sword in battle-fray.
I've slain men for a small thing,
And why not these, I pray?

Now I will tell you of my dream. Methought I went out of the homestead here by myself and without arms, and Thorarin seemed to come at me with a large whetstone in his hand, and I felt ill prepared for our meeting; but whilst I was thinking about it I saw another whetstone lying close by me, so I cuaght it up and attacked him, and when we met either tried to strike the other, but the two stones came against one another and there was a tremendous crash." "Was it such," asked Márr, "as might be considered a conflict between the two houses?" "More than that," replied Glum. "Did it seem that it might represent a conflict between the two districts?" "Yes," said Glum, "the omen may well be reckoned such, for I thought the crash could be heard all over the district, and when I woke I sung as follows

"I thought this night to see in sleep
that chief, who o'er the sea
guides the fierce raven of the deep,
Smite with a stone at me.

"The lord of Limafirth's broad strand
Came on in all his pride,
I met him fearless hand to hand
And dash'd the blow aside.

Márr observed it was very likely the old saying would come true, "Each of you will smite the other with and evil stone before it is over." "Yes," said Glum, "it is not improbable; there are many bodings tending that way. There is another dream to tell you. Methought I was standing out of doors, and that I saw two women who had a trough between them, and they took their stations at Hrisateig and sprinkled the whole district with blood. I woke up, and I think this portends something which is to happen. Then I sung these verses--

"The gods--methought, they swept along
Across the path of men.
the clash of swords and the javelin's song
We shall hear full soon again.

"I saw the maids of carnage stand,
In grim and vengeful mood,
As the battle rag'd, and they drench'd the land
In slaughter'd warriors blood."

That morning Márr rode to Mödrufell, with seventeen other men, to summon Arngrim for the death of Steinolf; but Glum remained at home with five men besides himself, and told them to be quick in getting back again. In the house with Glum were Jöd, and Eyiolf, the son of Thorleif the tall, Thorvald Tafalld, Glum's nephew, and two thralls.

# CHAPTER XXII.

HELGA, Glum's sister, who had been married to Steingrim of Sigluvik, had at that time come to Laugaland; she was the mother of Thorvald Tafalld, who was then eighteen years of age. There was a man named Thorvard, the son of Ornolf and of Yngvillda, who went by the name of "Everybody's sister." He lived at Krisnes, and had a son named Gudbrand, who was then twelve years old. Thorvard was a prudent man, and tolerably well inclined to help any one, but he was then old. That morning he was early a-foot, and told his man to get his horses. Then they rode to Thverà, and when they got there Márr had just started. Glum welcomed Thorvard well, and the latter inquired if any attempt had been made to procure a settlement between the parties. Glum told him "None." Thorvard asked, "Is the suit set on foot?" Glum said it was not. Then said the other, "A day like this would be a good one for this business: there is much mist, and no one would know what was going on, if one went quietly about it." Glum went on to say how matters stood, and how six men only remained at home. Thorvard answered, "You have rather a small number with you, but the steps you have taken will no doubt be sufficient." Then Thorvard rode to Espihole, and when he came thither the men were not up; but he found Thorarin, and inquired, "What do you intend to do? Do you intend to offer Glum any composition for the death?" Thorarin answered, "We do not think it an easy matter to offer to compound with Glum." "Is the suit set on foot?" asked Thorvard. "I have not heard," said Thorarin; "but what do you know about the matter?" "Oh," replied he, "Márr rode off this morning with seventeen others to proceed with the suit, and Glum remained at home with five men; no doubt it would now be a famous chance for setting matters straight, but you fellows here never get the best of it, because you are not so sharp in your movements as Glum is." "Well," said Thorarin, "the fact is I do not like to set up mere gossip and nonsense on our side to meet this charge." Thorvard answered, "Whether there was any sufficient cause or not is a point which ought to have been considered before Steinolf was killed. Did he not try to seduce Arngrim's wife? Of a surety I think such a matter as that is not to be reckoned as nothing." Thorarin persisted, "I do not like having to do with such a business." "What do you mean," said Thorvard, "by talking thus? Glum got something by that outlawry of your relative, Sigmund, and your clear course is not to let yourself be thus insulted by him." "I am not sure," said Thorarin, "whether that is or is not a wise course."

After this conversation the people of the house got up, and Thorvald the crooked pressed that they should ride to Upsal and give notice of outlawry as against Steinolf for his conduct to Arngrim's wife, so that he might be taken to have been rightly killed. Thorarin said, "That does not seem very advisable, but we will do it." There were fifteen of them in all, of whom seven are named, that is to say, Thorarin, Thorvald the crooked, his son Ketill, Arngrim, Eystein the Berserker, Thord the son of Rafn, who lived as Stockahlad, and had married Vigdis, the daughter of Thorir and widow of Sigmund, and Eyvind, the Norwegian who was staying with Thord. They went to Upsal, but Thorvard rode to Öngulstad (where there lived a good yeoman, Halli the fat), and sent his son to Thverà, desiring him to tell Glum the purpose of the men of Espihole, "and afterwards," he added, "you will ride back quickly to meet me."

When Thorvard came to Öngulstad, Halli asked what news he had to tell. "Nothing as yet," he replied; but then he told him what was the position of things, and Halli thought he saw pretty clearly that Thorvard had brought all this trouble on, and he told him that such men as he were born for mischief, inasmuch as he desired that every man should be at variance with his neighbour; and he added, "It would serve you right if you were killed." Then Halli went in a great hurry with all the people, men and women, whom he had got, with the intention of interfering between the two parties, if it were necessary. Gudbrand, Thorvard's son, got to Thverà, and said that his father had sent him thither; he told Glum what had occurred, and how "my father thought himself bound to tell you this which concerns you nearly, that the men of Espihole intend to give notice of outlawry as attaching to Steinolf." Glum's answer was, "Why did not your father come himself?" The lad said, "I consider it all the same which of us two came." Glum replied, "Your father has done well in sending you hither, if we are in want of men:" so he made him dismount, and fastened up his horse. Gudbrand exclaimed, "My father told me I must get back quickly." "Oh," rejoined Glum, "it cannot be so; he was desirous, no doubt, that you should show your manhood to-day."

In the meantime Thorvard began to say, "My son Gudbrand is late." Halli inquired whither he had sent him. "I sent him to Thverà," answered Thorvard. "It is well," said Halli, "that you should meet with some cunning people, and it serves you right."

The men of Espihole rode across the river with the intention of passing at the "Ship-ford." Glum saw them riding, and remarked that Márr was somewhat too late. Then he ran out of the homestead with six men, of whom Gudbrand was one, and followed the other party. He had his shield and a halberd, with his sword by his side, and hastened on the road, with his men after him, to come up with them. When Thorarin saw them coming he had his people ride their own way, no faster and no slower on that account, "and no one can blame us for that." Thord, the son of Rafn, asked Thorarin whether they with twenty men were to let themselves be chased by Glum with his six? Thorarin's answer was, "Let us ride on, for Glum's object is to delay us and to wait for his own people." Thord said, "It is no wonder that when he stands on equal vantage-ground with us we often get the worst of it with Glum; seeing that now, when he has only a few men with him, you do not dare to wait for him; but he shall not make me run," and so he dismounted. Eystein the Berserker said too that he would not ride away from Glum, "so that they should profess to have driven us off." Thorarin observed that this course seemed to him inexpedient; but when Glum saw that they did not go on, he slackened his pace, and addressed Thorarin, asking what their errand was at Upsal. Thorarin replied that they had determined to proclaim Steinolf as liable to outlawry. Then Glum said, "Is not this rather too strong a measure? Should not some offer of satisfaction be tried first, and we might possibly hit upon some method for bringing this suit to a close." Thorarin said that he wanted to delay them and had them ride on, and so they did. Glum asked them, "Will you stay a little bit longer?" but they rode away from him, and as they rode slower, so Glum slackened his pace and waited for his men, and said, "Your cause will not find much favour, if you rake up a parcel of lies, and it will end only in disgrace." "We shall not look to that now," replied Thorarin; "it is a hard matter to come to terms with you." Whilst they rode on, Glum kept going forward alongside of them, talking with them, and thus delayed them. But when he saw he could not keep them back any longer, and felt sure of his own men coming up, then he threw his spear at Arngrim so that it went through the man's thigh and the saddle-bow also, and Arngrim was disabled for the day. Eystein was the first who then rushed at Glum, but Thorvald Tafalld stood out to meet him, and they two fought with each other. Every other man thought he was well off in proportion as he kept away from them; for they were both full of courage and strength, and each of them dealt the other many and sore strokes. Thorvald the crooked attacked

Glum sharply and many more with him, but Glum and his men got out of their way and protected themselves as well as they could. Thorarin did not get off his horse, for he thought that they were quite enough to set on one man."

# CHAPTER XXIII.

WHILST they were fighting a man came up at full speed, wearing a hood of skins, with a sword in his hand. He came where Thorvald Tafalld had fallen before Eystein, and rushing at the latter, gave him a death-blow. Then he joined himself to Glum's side, and Glum called out to him, "Good luck to you Thundarbenda! I made a good bargain when I bought you. You will pay me well to-day for the outlay." Now Glum had a thrall who was called by that name, and that is why he spoke thus; but in reality it was Vigfuss, Glum's son, though few or none except Glum himself knew him, for he had been three winters outlawed and living in concealment, so that most people thought he had gone abroad. It happened that whilst Glum was getting away he fell, and lay on the ground, and his two thralls lay over him, and were killed with spear-thrusts; but at that moment Márr with his men came up. Then Thorarin got off his horse, and he and Márr fought, without any other men meddling with them. Glum sprung up, and joined heartily in the fight, and there was then no advantage of number on either side. A servant of Thorarin's, named Eirik, who had been about his work in the morning, came too his mater's aid with a club in his hand, but without other arms of offence of defence; and Glum suffered much by him because his men were injured both in person and in their arms by that club which he bore. It is told too that Halldor, Glum's wife, called on the women to go with her, saying, "We will bind up the wounds of those men who have any hope of life, whichever party they belong to." When she came up Thorarin was just struck down by Márr, his shoulder was cut away in such fashion that the lungs were exposed. But Halldor bound up his wound, and kept watch over him till the fight was over.

Halli the fat was the first who came up to interfere, and may men were with him. The end of the combat was that five men of those from Espihole were killed, that is to say, Thorvald the crooked, Arngrim, Eysein, Eirik, and Eyvind the Norwegian. On Glum's side there fell Thorvald Tafalld, Eyiolf son of Thorleif, Jöd, and the two thralls. Thorarin got home with his people; Glum also returned with his men, and had the dead carried into an outbuilding, where the utmost honour was done to the body of Thorvald, for garments were placed under it, and it was sewn up in a skin. When the men had returned, Glum said to Halldora, "Our expedition to-day would have been successful, if you had staid at home, and if Thorarin had not escaped with his life." She replied, There is little of life in Thorarin, and if he lives you will not be able to remain in the district long; but if he dies you will not be able to remain in the country at all." After this Glum said to Gudbrand, "You got much honour by your prowess to-day in killing Thorvald the crooked, and you did us good service." Gudbrand replied that nothing of the sort had happened; he had only defended himself as well as he could. "Oh," said Glum, "that is all very well. I saw clearly what took place; a mere child in age to kill such a champion as Thorvald! You will always be talked of for this deed. I got credit abroad in the same way for killing the Berserker." "I never slew Thorvald," answered Gudbrand. "It is no use trying to conceal it, my good friend, you gave him the wound which killed him. Do not shirk the good luck which has fallen to you." Glum maintained his point with Gudbrand till the latter believed what he said, admitted that he had done it, and thought it an honour to himself, so that it could no longer be concealed, and the death was formally laid to his charge. This seemed to those who took up the suit for Thorvald's slaughter to be less promising than had been expected: Thorvald was chosen as the man whose death was to be avenged.

People report a speech of Glum's--"One thing I do not like, and that is that Márr should have his head tied up, though he has gat a bump on it." What he called "a bump" was in fact a cut crosswise over his head. Márr's answer was, "I should not need this so much if I had lain down and use a couple of thralls as a shield." "Well, my lad," said Glum, "our field Hrisateig (Bush acre) was hard to mow to-day." Márr replied, "It will turn out a bad mowing for you in one way, for you have mowed the land at Thverà out of your own hands." "I do not think you know that for a certainty," rejoined Glum. "I may not know it, but it will turn out for you as if I did now it," was Márr's answer. Now, when Helga, Glum's sister, heard the tidings, she came over to Thverà and asked how her son had borne himself. "There was no better man," said Glum. "I should like to see him dead," said she, "if that is all that is left for me." they allowed her to do so, and she caused him to be lifted into the waggon, and tenderly handled, and when she got home she cleansed his wounds and bound them up, and dealt with him in such a way that he recovered his speech.

The law was then that if an equal number of men were killed on either side they were set off against each other, though there might be a difference in the men themselves; but if one party had the worst of it they had to select the man for whom atonement was to be demanded. If anything however, happened to turn up afterwards, by which it would have seemed better to have made a different choice, they could not change their selection. When Thorarin heard that Thorvald Tafalld was alive, he chose his own brother Thorvald the crooked, as the man to be atoned for. When, however, he found a little afterwards that the latter's death was laid to the charge of Gudbrand, he would gladly have selected another man, but he had to abide by his first choice. Then they found Einar the son of Eyiolf, and Thorarin told him he should now take advantage of that agreement which they had formerly made with each other. Einar replied, "My mind is the same now that it was formerly when Bárd was killed." he then took up the suit to carry it on at the Thing, in the summer, and he made the charge against Glum. Thorarin was laid up with his wounds the whole summer, and so was Thorvald Tafalld, but they both recovered. Glum had a great number of men with him at the Thing, and so in fact had both parties. An attempt was now made by persons of consideration connected with both sides to bring about a settlement of the case. The suit was compounded on these conditions, that is to say, that the death of Steinolf was to be considered as atoned for, if Vigfuss, Glum's son, were proclaimed free from his penalty. Gudbrand, however, was convicted of the death of Thorvald, and Glum got him taken abroad. They returned home with affairs in this condition; but Thorvard and Thorarin were very much dissatisfied, and the latter thought he had obtained no honourable satisfaction for the death of his brother Thorvald. Glum remained at home much looked up to, and in the course of the winter there got abroad a stanza which he had lately composed:

She asks--he nymph that pours the wine--
the deeds of death that I have done.
They're past and gone, those deeds of mine;
But no man yet has talked of one. [1]

_______________________________

[1] There are four other lines in the original text, but they are so corrupt and obscure that I cannot venture to paraphrase them.

# CHAPTER XXIV.

ONE day, when men had got together at the warm bath of Hrafnagil, Thorvard came thither. He was a merry fellow, and amused himself in many ways. "What men," he asked, "have you got here who can entertain us with some fresh stories?" "There is plenty of amusement and fun where you are," they said. "Well," he replied, "nothing amuses me more than reciting Glum's verses; but I keep thinking over what can be the faulty reckoning he speaks of in one of his stanzas, when he says he did not get credit for all the people he had killed. What are we to suppose to be the real state of the case? Which is more likely, that Gudbrand killed Thorvald, or that Glum did it?" This view seemed to many men worth consideration, and Thorvard rode to meet Thorarin, and said to him, "I have been thinking the matter out, and I am convinced that the truth has not been known about the death of Thorvald the crooked. You will find in Glum's verses, that he says he has not got credit for all the men he has killed." Thorarin answered, "I can hardly take the case up again, though you should be right, and so things shall remain as they are." Thorvard rejoined, "That is not a proper course, although if the matter had not been revived, all might have gone on quietly; no I shall talk of it publicly, and there will fall on you disgrace greater than any which has yet ensued in this affair." "Well," said Thorarin, "it seems to me an awkward matter to carry this cause to the Althing, in the face of the power of Glum and his kinsmen." Thorvard replied," I can give you a piece of advice on that point. Summon him to the Hegranes Thing: you have plenty of kinsmen there, and he will find it hard to defend the case." "That we will do," said Thorarin, an so they parted.

The spring was a bad one, and everything became difficult to procure. At that time Thorarin set on foot the suit as against Glum at Hegranes Thing, inasmuch as all the priests of the different division in the district who belonged to that Thing, were bound to Thorarin by the ties of kindred. It was scarcely possible to get across the moors with horses, on account of the snow. So Glum adopted the plan of putting a large vessel into the charge of his brother, Thorstein, who was to sail in her to the westward, and convey arms and provisions to the Thing. When, however, they came off Ulfsdal, the ship went to pieces, and all the men and property on board her were lost. Glum got to the Thing with a hundred and twenty men, but he could not encamp nearer to the place itself than in the outer circle, or "verge" of the court. [1] Einar, the son of Eyiolf, with the men of Espihole, was already there. Word was sent to Glum that he was to present himself to the court, and produce his plea in answer to the indictment. Glum went accordingly, but the men were drawn up on both sides in such a way that there was not more space than would allow of one man passing, and Glum was desired to go into the enclosure if he wanted to get to the court. He did not think this an advisable course, so he said to his men, "It is easy to see that they think they have got our affair in their own hands now. Well, it may be so, but I should like you to fall back and change your order. I will march first, then two men following me in a line, and then four in a line after them, and so on; and we will march right at them, keeping our spears before us, and this sort of wedge must make its way in if you follow

---

[1] I believe that the word in the original "Fiörbaugsgardr' occurs only twice in the sense of the verge or ring round the ground on which the Thing met. Mr. Dasent speaks of it as "an enclosed space near a court, a 'verge', or 'liberty,' within which the Fiörbaugsmadr (that is one liable to the lesser outlawry) was safe." See preface to the Nial's Saga, p. clxii.

close up. They did this, and pushed without interruption right into the ring which was cleared for the court, but it was night long before they could be got of the ground again, so as to allow the court to sit; so great was the crush and press. At last it was brought about that the court was reconstituted, and they were proceeding to sum up the case when Glum came forward on the bank were the court was held, and called his witnesses to the fact that the sun had risen again on the field of the Thing; then he protested solemnly against any judgment being given in the case before them. It followed from this protest that every suit before the court at once discontinued and fell to the ground. Men rode away, and the people of Espihole were very ill pleased with what had happened. [1]

Thorarin declared that Glum had dealt vexatiously with them, but Einar replied, "The matter does not appear to me to be so very ugly, for the suit may be taken up again at the point where it left off." Afterwards the men of Espihole rode to the Althing with Einar, and with many of their friends who had promised them their support against glum. Glum's kinsmen gave him their help also in securing the benefit of the point of law, and the matter was settled by the advice of skilled men, on condition that Glum would take an oath in the case to the effect that he did not kill Thorvald the crooked. So when many men interceded, they compounded the matter on these terms--that Glum should swear he had not slain him; and the time was appointed when the oath should be taken, that is to say, in the autumn, five weeks before winter. They followed up the suit with such vigour that they were determined to bring it on again, if he did not take the necessary oath in three temples on the Eyjafirth,

---

[1] The reason for this seems to be that the defendant was summoned to answer on a certain day, and when the sun rose again before he was formally called on, that day was over, and the whole proceedings were avoided.

and if it were not done at the prescribed time the right to clear himself by the oath was to be forfeited. There was much talk about this business, and what Gum's oaths would be, and how he would get on with them.

# CHAPTER XXV.

NOW men returned from the Thing, and Glum staid at home all the summer: everything was quiet in the district till it came to the time of the "Leet," [1] when they assembled at that court. Glum, however, was not there, and nothing was heard of him. Márr was at home in his dwelling; but in the autumn, five weeks before winter, he held a wedding-feast, and invited men to it, so that not less than a hundred and twenty people came together. This invitation appeared strange to everybody, for those who were concerned in the wedding were not persons of any consequence. That evening all the men of Eyjafirth were seen riding in from the dales two or five at a time, and the people who came down into the district were all collected in one body. Glum was there, and Asgrim, and Gizor, with three hundred and sixty men, and they came in the course of the night to the homestead, and sat at the wedding-feast.

The morning after Glum sent to find Thorarin, and told him to come to Diupadal, not later than six in the morning, to hear the oaths. Thorarin bestirred himself and got together a hundred and twenty men, and when they came to the temple, six people went into it, that is to say, Gizor and Asgrim with Glum, and Einar and Hlenni the old with Thorarin. Whoever had to take the

---

[1] The Haust-thing, or autumn assembly, was the same as the Leid or Leet, and was held not earlier than fourteen days after the Althing, for the purpose of making known in each district what had been done at the general assembly. It had, like every other Thing, to be helgad, "consecrated," or opened by the Godi. See Maurer, ss. 171-174; Dasent, Preface, p. lxvi.

"temple oath" laid hold with his hand of the silver ring, which was stained red with the blood of the cattle sacrificed, and which ought not to weigh less than three ounces. Then Glum said word for word thus: "I name Asgrim to bear witness, and Gizor in the second place to bear witness, that I take the 'temple oath,' on the ring, and I say it to the God. [1] When Thorvald the crooked got his death-blow--Vark at þar--ok vák ek þar--ok raudk at þ odd ok egg. Now let those men who are skilled in such matters, and who stand by, look to my oath." [2]

---

[1] The god probably means Thor. See Maurer, § 157.

[2] It is impossible to represent this oath of Glum's in English, or any other language, so as to make the point of the story clear; but it may thus be explained--There is in the Icelandic language, or rather there was, and enelitic negative at (sometimes abbreviated to a or t), which is attached to the verb. It occurs only in the ancient tongue, and there only in poetry and legal formulæ. Thus var ek or vark means simply "I was," ek being the pronoun of the first person; but vark-at means "I was not." So vák (or vá ek) means "I slew;" but vák-at means "I slwe not." But at is also a preposition corresponding to our preposition "at," and vark at, pronounced as two separate words (with the accent on at) would mean "I was at it." the reader will thus see that the deceit practised by Glum consisted in so pronouncing the verb and the particle at, that his enemies took it for the negative and not for the preposition. The sense depended entirely on the question whether it was or was not an enclitic. Glum's adversaries understood him to say, "I was not there; I slew him not there; I reddened not edge nor point on him there;" whereas his own construction of what he swore to was precisely the opposite and in fact expressly asserted his guilt. The whole of this story is most curious as illustrative of the manner and character of the people, and also in a philological point of view. The reader who wishes to know more of the extinct negative suffix may consult Grimm's Grammar, b. iii. s. 715. Grimm is mistaken in saying that this form occurs only in the old poetry, as is sufficiently shown by this very Saga; but it is confined to the poetry and the laws. I may add that Grimm's attempt, at p. 718, to explain the origin of this negative appears to me unsuccessful. I shall have occasion to remark hereafter

Thorarin and his friends were not prepared to find any fault, but they said they had never heard the form of words used before. In the same manner the oaths were taken by Glum at Gnupafell and at Thverà. Gizor and Asgrim stayed some nights at Thverà, and when they went away Glum gave Gizor the blue cloak, and he gave Asgrim the gold-mounted spear (which Vigfuss had given him). [1] In the course of the winter Thorvard met Thorarin, and asked him, "Did Glum take the oath properly?" "We found nothing to take hold of," said Thorarin. "It is a wonderful thing," replied Thorvard, "that wise people should make such mistakes. I have known men who have declared themselves to have slain others, but I have never known a case of a man swearing explicitly that he was guilty, as Glum did. How could he say more than he did when he declared that he was there at the doing of the deed, that he took part in the death, and that he reddened point and edge, when Thorvald the crooked fell at Hrisateig?--though I admit that he did not pronounce the words as they are commonly pronounced. That scandal will never be done away with." Thorarin replied, "I did not observe this, but I am tired of having to do with Glum." "Well," said Thorvard, "if you are tired because your health is not equal to it, let Einar take the matter up. He is a prudent man, with a great kindred, and many will follow him. His brother Gudmund will not be neutral, and he himself is most anxious for one thing-to get to Thverà." Then they met Einar and consulted with him, and Thorarin said, "If you will take the lead in the suit many men will back you in it, and we will bring it about that you shall have Glum's land, at a price not exceeding that which he paid to Thorkel the tall." Einar observed, "Glum has now parted with

---

that this oath of Glum's was not in itself part of a judicial proceeding, but was imposed upon him as a special condition of an exceptional character, when his adversaries agreed to compound their suit.

[1] See above, chapter vi. The parting with these gifts is the turning-point in Glum's story. Henceforth his luck is departed.

those two things, his cloak and his spear, which his mother's father, Vigfuss, gave him, and bad him keep, if he wished to hold his position, telling him that he would fall away in dignity from the time that he let them out of his hands. Now will I take up the suit and follow it out."

# CHAPTER XXVI.

EINAR now set the suit on foot afresh for the Althing, and both sides collected their people together, but before Glum left home he dreamt that many persons came to Thverà to visit the god Frey, and he thought he saw a great crowd on the sandbanks by the river, with Frey sitting on a chair. He dreamt that he asked who they were who had come thither, and they said, "We are thy departed kindred, and we are now begging Frey that thou may'st not be driven out of Thverà, but it is no use, for he answers shortly and angrily, and calls to mind now the gift of the ox by Thorkel the tall." At that point Glum woke up, and ever afterwards he professed that he was on worse terms with Frey.

Men rode to the Thing, and the suit was brought to a close in such a way that Glum admitted the killing of Thorvald; but his kinsmen and friends exerted themselves to secure the acceptance of a settlement rather than the imposition of outlawry or banishment. So they compounded the matter at the Thing, on the condition that Glum was to forfeit the land at Thverà, half absolutely as an atonement to Ketell, the son of Thorvald the crooked, and to convey the other half at a valuation; but he was allowed to live there till the spring, and was then to be outlawed in the district, and not to live nearer than in Hörgardal. So they left the Thing. Einar afterwards bought the land, as had been promised to him. In the spring his men came thither to work on the farm, and Einar told them that they should give an account to him of every word which Glum spoke. One day he came and talked with them on this wise, "It is easy to see that Einar has got good workmen about him; the work is well done on the land, and it is now of consequence that great and little matters should both be attended to. You would do well to put up posts here by the water side for drying clothes; it is convenient for the women washing the larger articles; the wells at home are indifferent."

When they got home Einar asked what Glum had said to them. They told him how careful he was with reference to all the work done. "Did it appear to you," said he, "that he was desirous of getting everything ready for my hands?" "Yes," they replied, "so we think." "Well," replied Einar, "I think differently. I think he meant very likely to hang you on these posts, or stick on them some insult to me. You must not go there, however."

Einar transferred his household to Thverà in the spring, but Glum remained where he was till the last day for moving, [1] and when people were all ready to start he sat down on the high seat and did not move, although he was summoned to do so. He had the hall decorated with hangings, and refused to turn out like mere "cottage tenants." Hallbera, the daughter of Thorodd, the son of Hialm, was the mother of Gudmund and Einar, and lived at Hanakamb. She came to Thverà, and saluted Glum, saying, "Good morning to you, Glum, but you cannot stay here any longer. I have marked out the land of Thverà with fire, and I eject you and all yours formally from it, as made over to my son Einar." [2] Then Glum rose up and told her she might chatter

---

[1] The last of the "flitting days"--Fardagar. They began on the Thursday after the expiration of six weeks of summer, which was reckoned to begin on the Thursday between the 9th and 15th of April. They fell therefore about the beginning of June. See the Glossary to the Grágás, and Dasent's Preface, p. liv.

[2] Maurer (s. 58) gives a translation of this curious passage, and remarks that it shows the hallowing of the land by fire as applicable not only to its first occupation, but also to a change of possession.

away like a miserable old woman as she was; but as he rode away he looked over his shoulder towards the homestead and sung a stanza--

With sword and spear, as fame hath told,
Like many a gallant earl of old,
I won these lands by might and main.
But now the wielder of the brand
Has dash'd at last from out his hand,
Broad lands and lordships lost again.

Glum lived at Mödrufell, in Hörgardal, with Thorgrim Fiuk, but he was not content to remain there more than one winter. Then he dwelt two winters in Myrkárdal, but a landslip fell near the homestead and destroyed some of the buildings. After that he bought land at Thverbrek, in Öxnadal, and dwelt there as long as he lived, and became aged and blind. [1]

---

[1] Some verses of Glum's occur here, but the text is so doubtful that I cannot venture a translation of them.

# CHAPTER XXVII.

THERE was a man named Narvi who dwelt at Hrisey. He had as his wife Ulfeida, the daughter of Ingiald, son of Helgi the thin. Their sons were Eyiolf, Klængr, Thorbrand, and Thorvald, all distinguished men and kinsmen of Glum's. Two of these, Klæengr and Eyiolf, lived at Hrisey, after their father's death. A man named Thorvald, who had married Helga, the daughter of Thord, the son of Hraf, of Stöckahlad, and who was nicknamed "Menni," dwelt at Hagi at that time. One spring Thorvald came from Hagi, and lay off Hrisey in his vessel, intending to fish, and when Klængr was aware of this he stared with him. They got out into the firth, and fell in with a whale which was just dead, which they made fast and towed into the firth in the course of the day. Klængr wanted to bring the carcass into Hrisey, because the distance was shorter, but Thorvald desired to tow it to Hagi, and said he had and equal right to do so. Klængr maintained that it was not the law to take it anywhere except to the nearest point where any of the men engaged in the capture owned land. Thorvald asserted his rights, and said that Glum's kinsmen had no business to interfere with the fair partition of the fish. Whatever the laws were, the strongest should now have their way. At that moment Thorvald had the largest number of men with him, and so they took the drift fish from Klængr by force, though both of them were land-owners. Klængr went home very much dissatisfied, and Thorvald and his people laughed at him and his party, telling them they did not dare to hold on to their booty.

One morning Klængr got up early, and went with three other men in to Hagi, so as to be there in good time whilst people were still asleep. Then Klængr said--"We'll try a scheme; here are cattle about in the homestead; we will drive them on to the buildings, under which Thorvald is asleep, and so we shall get him to come out." [1] They did this, and Thorvald woke up and rushed out of doors. Klængr made at him, and gave him a mortal wound; but went away again without daring to declare himself the slayer, because there were so many people about on the spot. So he went out to one of the islands, and there declared that he had killed Thorvald. The right of claiming atonement belonged to Thorarin and Thord, and they treated the case as one of murder. [2] When the suit was being brought before the Thing, Glum was quiet at home, but whilst the Thing was going on he went about in the districts of Fliot and Svarvadardal, begging for help to meet the execution of the anticipated sentence of forfeiture; however, he asked men to say nothing of this intention of his. Klaufi, of Bárd, exclaimed, "To be sure we will help Glum; he married Halldora, the daughter of Arnor Red-cheek;" and many men besides promised to support him. Then Glum returned home, but the suit ran its course at the Thing, and when that was over they got ready to carry out the sentence of forfeiture with four ships, and thirty men in each ship. Einar, Thorarn, and Thord commanded the ships, and when they came in-shore at the island, in the twilight of morning, they saw a smoke rising over the buildings. Einar asked his people whether it appeared to them, as it did to him, that the smoke was not a clear blue. They answered that so it seemed to them. "Then," said Einar, "it appears likely to me from that smoke that there are a good many people in the house, and that steam hanging in the air must be the steam from men. If this be so we shall find out about it by rowing away from the island openly and then we shall be sure if there by any

---

[1] The caves must have been level with the ground and probably covered with turf or sod.
[2] Because the slayer had not on the spot avowed the deed.

number of men there." They did this, and when the men who were in the island saw them they rushed out to their vessels, and put out after them, for Glum had come thither with two hundred and forty men, and they chased them right up to Oddaeyr, so that the sentence of forfeiture was not carried out, and the men of Eyjafirth got dishonour by the failure.

Glum remained in his own dwelling through the summer. He had to open an Autumn court; but the place of holding it is on the east of the firth, not far from Kaupáng, and the men of Eyjafirth got a large force together, whilst Glum had only thirty men. Many people spoke to Glum and told him that he ought not to go with a small number of followers. His answer was, "The finest portion of my life is gone by, and I am pleased that they have not driven me so hard that I cannot ride the straight path." He went up the firth in a ship, and then disembarked and went to he booths. Now between the firth and the booths there are certain steep ascents covered with loose gravel, and when Glum came opposite to the booth which belonged to Einar, men rushed out upon him and his people and dashed their shields against them so as to push them down the slope. Glum fell and rolled shield and all down the bank on to the spit of sand below. He was not wounded, but three spears had stuck in his shield. Thorvald Tafalld had then come to shore and saw that Glum was in a strait: he jumped on land with his oar in his hand and, running up the slope, hurled it at Gudmund the powerful: it came against his shield, which broke, and the handle of the oar struck him on the breast so that he fell down senseless and was carried off by four men to his booth. Then they challenged one another to come on, and cast weapons and stones on both sides, and the contest was a hard one; many were wounded; but all said the same thing--that it was impossible for a small number to fight better than Glum and his men had done. Einar and his men made a vigorous onslaught; but people interfered,

and it ended in Glum losing two men, Klængr, the son of Narvi,
and Grim Eyrarlegg, the brother of his wife Halldora. Then Brusi,
the son of Halli, made these verses:

"Thou warrior-goddess of the shield!
We held our own in battle fray--
I know 'tis so--we did not yield
The honour of the day.

"Those chiefs forsooth, the while we fought,
(Bright nymph! it may not be denied)
Strode somewhat faster than I though
Adown the steep hill side."

Then Einar composed a stanza:

"he had to run away perforce
From out the fight--that swordsman bold--
I trow 'twas hard to stop his course
As down the bank he roll'd.

"Well us'd the pirate's spear to wield,
In vain that chieftain fought,
And the loose shingle fail'd to yield
The foothold which he sought."

Then Glum composed some verses in answer to him:

"Though standing on the band so high
Their helmets made a gallant show,
They did not dare their luck to try
Upon the beach below.

"They did not dare to risk the path,
Whilst on the sandy shore we stood,

And fac'd the dread Valkyrie's wrath
With shields that dripp'd with blood."

The matter was settled upon the ground that the death of Klængr and Thorvald of Hagi were set off one against the other, and the slaying of Grim Eyrarlegg was considered equal to the injury caused to Gudmund; but Glum was much dissatisfied with this close of the suit, as he expressed himself in the following stanza, which he made afterwards:

"The world is worthless; and my life
With all the keen delights of strife
Hath well-nigh passed away.

"Too weak, when gallant Grim lay low,
To strike 'mid men th' avenging blow,
And blood with blood repay!"

# CHAPTER XXVIII.

IT happened one summer that the brothers Gudmund and Einar were riding back from the Thing, when Glum invited some guests to his house, and he sent men up to Öxnadal-heath and asked those brothers also, professing that he wished to be reconciled to them wholly and entirely. "For," said he, "on account of old age I am fit for nothing, and I will not invite them only to a meal." Glum was then blind, but he caused a look-out to be kept for their coming. Gudmund wished to accept the invitation, but Einar did not; and each of them rode on his own side of the river, till Glum was told that one of the two troops was coming that way. "Then," said he, "Einar will not accept the invitation; he is so distrustful that he will put confidence in no man." It is reported that Einar called out to Gudmund and said, "If you go thither this evening, I will be sure to be there tomorrow;" but Gudmund reflected on those words and said, "Well, you must mean that you will have to take measures for avenging my death;" and so he turned round and followed Einar. It was told to Glum that neither of the two was coming. "Then it is a bad business," exclaimed he, "for if I had gone to meet them, I had made up my mind not to miss both of them." He had a drawn sword under his cloak. So this was the last thing which passed between Glum and the men of Eyjafirth.

When Christianity was introduced in these parts Glum was baptized, and lived three winters afterwards. He was confirmed in his last illness by Bishop Kol, and died in white vestments. Márr, Glum's son, lived at Forn-Hagi, and caused a church to be built there, in which Glum and Márr himself, when he died, were buried. Many other people also were buried there, because for a long time there was but that one church in Hörgárdal. People relate that for twenty years Glum was the greatest chief on Eyjafirth; and for another twenty years there were no greater men there, though some were on an equal footing with him. They say too that of all the valiant men that have been in this land he had the noblest spirit. And so ends the Story of Glum.

# SUPPLEMENTARY NOTE

## On Judicial Proceedings on the Holmgang, and Appeal for Murder

WHEN I first read the account of Hallvard's trial in Chapter xviii, in my ignorance of Icelandic law, I conceived it to be a case of acquittal by "compurgators," as in our old "Wager of Law." I soon found, however, that this view was entirely erroneous. Trial by compurgators, curiously enough, was unknown to the law of Iceland. Schlegel, in his preface to the Grágás (Copenhagen, 1829), says, Consacramentalium autem nullus usus apud Islando obtinuit; quod eo magis mirum quum iis cæteræ gentes Semptemtrionales olim æquè ac aliæ medio ævo sæpe uterentur" (p. lxxxiv.).

In his prface to the Nial's Saga, Mr. Dasent has described, with great detail, the manner in which the four great inquests of thirty-six householders each were constituted for the four quarter courts at the Althing, but the mode of trial described in the text is one entirely different from the Buakvidr, and was called the "Tolftarkvidr." In it the judgment was given by a verdict of the Godi, or priest, with eleven other members of his district. If we are at liberty to apply the rules laid down in the Grágás to the earlier period of this story, the following particulars may be stated--

The Godi himself named the eleven other men, nor does it seem to have been necessary that they should be householders. This inquest might be challenged, and if they did not agree the majority decided. If they were equally divided that side prevailed on which the Godi voted (Grágás. Thingskapathátr, ch. vii-xvii.). It will thus be seen that practically the case was in the hands of the Godi, and Hallvard's fate depended on Glum acting in that capacity; by the Buakvidr his well-known character would probably have secured a verdict against him.

In the Eyrbyggia Saga a complicated case occurs. Geirrid, the sister of Arnkel, himself a Godi, is charged by Thorbiörn with having bewitched his son Gunnlaug. Snorri, another Godi, was the brother-in-law of Thorbiörn, and supported the charge made by the latter. Neither Arnkel nor Snorri therefore, being respectively thus connected with the accuser and accused, were considered competent to decide the case by the Tolftarkvidr. Accordingly a third Godi, Helgi, was called in, but Arnkel was allowed to swear on the altar-ring (Stalla-hring) that Geirrid was innocent, and Thorarin swore with ten men, I presume, the other way. Then Helgi acquitted Geirrid (Eyrbyggia Saga, c. xxi.). In this case Arnkel and Thorarin seem to be something between compurgators and witnesses, but the verdict is given by another. The Tolftarkvidr, therefore, in Halvard's case was neither like our "wager of law" nor like the verdict of a jury.

I have already observed that Glum's oath of purgation, in chapter xxv., seems to be a case of an exceptional character, dependent on a special compact between the parties. The accusers agreed to a compromise only on the express condition that he should take such an oath, and it must be remembered that another person had already been declared guilty of the death with which he was charged. We are told, at the end of chapter xxiv. that it was on this condition alone the suit was to drop; the oath itself was no part of the proceedings in such suit.

With regard to the Holmgang or duel as a recognized method for terminating a suit, Maurer tells us that it was supposed to be abolished in Iceland in 1011, very few years after the introduction by Nial of the Fifth Court at the Althing, but I confess hat I doubt whether its abolition was so closely connected as he supposes with the institution of this tribunal. In the first place the cases provided for by the Fifth Court in which legal proceedings would previously have been brought to a dead lock, were only a portion, and a small portion, of those in which the Holmgang might naturally be resorted to. In the second place, moreover, we learn that it was in like manner abolished in Norway, in 1012, by Eric, the son of Hakon, without any such supplementary court being instituted to supply its place. [1] I am more inclined to think that the influence of Christianity, and a gradual change in the manners of the people led to an alteration in both countries, and that the same feeling showed the necessity of additional judicial facilities in Iceland. Of course I admit that the institution of the Fifth Court would have a tendency to diminish the number of cases in which men would have recourse to the Holmgang.

In the face of these facts and dates, it is a curious question for an Englishman--"When was the duel as a recognised part of a judicial process abolished in England?" The answer is, in the year 1818! So that in this reform we were 800 years behind our kinsmen in Iceland and Scandinavia.

This subject is interesting in itself, and I am the more tempted to dwell on it because the analogy between the old laws of England and Iceland is very strong and in some points illustrates forcibly that confusion between prosecutions and private suits which makes it sometimes difficult to use what would now be appropriate legal language with reference to transactions narrated in the text.

---

[1] See Grettir's Saga, chap. xix.

In an appeal for murder, as it existed in England at Common Law, the relative had the right to proceed; a right designated in Iceland by the word "Eptirmál," and which there could be handed over before witnesses from one man to another.

In England, by an ordinance of Henry I., this right was confined to the four first degrees of blood. In 1297, by the Great Charter of Edward I., it was further limited in the case of women. "Nullus capiatur aut imprisonetur propter appellum femine de morte alterius quam viri sui" (Recort Statutes, vol. i. p 118) In the Eyrbyggia Saga we learn that in consequence of the unsatisfactory manner in which the women, to whom the Eptirmál for a certain Arnkel belonged, had prosecuted the suit, a law was made by the "Landstiórnamenn" (that is, I suppose, the Lögretta or Legislative Committee of the Althing) to the effect that women and minors below sixteen should no longer have the Eptirmál (Eyrbyggia, Leipzig, 1864, p. 69). By our statute of Glouchester (6, Edward I., c. 9, 1278) it was provided that appeals should not abate as easily as had previously been the case, but that if the appellor set forth the deed, the day, the hour, the time of the king, the town where the deed was done, and the weapon, the appeal should not abate for want of fresh suit, provided it was made within the year and day after the deed.

It does not follow that this limitation of a year and a day was then established for the first time (See Blackstones, Comm., iv. p. 315). I ought to observe that the clause referred to above from the statute of Glouchester is printed in the Record Edition of the Statutes from M. 3, Cott. Vesp. B. vii. fol. 24, 6, and is not in the copy in the Tower Rolls or in many other copies of the Act.

By the 3rd of Henry Vii., c. 2 (1487), a great change was made in the proceeding on appeals for murder.

Lord Bacon, in his history of that king, tells us: "There was also made another law for peace in general, and repressing of murders and manslaughters, and was in amendment of the Common Laws of the realm; being this; That whereas by the Common Law the King's suit, in case of homicide, did expect the year and the day, allowed to the party's suit by way of appeal; and that it was found by experience that the party was many times compounded with, and many times wearied with the suit, so that in the end such suit was let fall, and by that time the matter was in a manner forgotten, and thereby prosecution at the King's suit by indictment (which is ever the best) flagrante crimine neglected; it was ordained, at any time within the year and the day as after; not prejudicing nevertheless the party's suit." Southey (Common Place Book, iii. p 8) justly remarks that this was the first step towards giving public justice preference over private. By the words "not prejudicing the party's suit," Lord Bacon means that the accused, if acquitted, ought still to be detained in prison or bailed until the year and day had expired, so that the appeal might yet be made by the relatives in spite of the acquittal. Accordingly Sir Thomas Smith, in his (Commonwealth of England," describes both processes by indictment and appeal as still existing; and in 1818, after a prisoner had been acquitted by a jury for the murder of Mary Ashford, the brother of the deceased appealed the defendant in open court. In consequence of this case the whole proceeding by appeal and wager of battle was abolished by the Statute 59, George III., c. 46.

The history of this single point of our criminal law is eminently characteristic of the way in which our institutions work. The practical evils and inconveniences connected with appeals were remedied, as they arose, in the reigns of Edward I. and Henry

Vii., but no one ventured to touch the general principle. In fact, in the latter reign, it is clear that the whole proceeding was really out of date, but instead of suppressing it, the legislature contented itself with giving priority to the king's suit, and allowed it to slumber on. All of a sudden, three hundred years afterwards, it is discovered to be alive, and men are startled by its reappearance as much as they would be if one of the mailed barons of those days were now to rise from his tomb in the Abbey, and stalk across to take his seat in the House of Lords. That at last it is really abolished.